ASTAROTH

A Coralie Westerly Story

Chris Regan

CONTENTS

FOREWORD

I first discovered the writings of Coralie West-erly on her now defunct blog, Stories the Dead Told Me. The blog wasn't much to look at, just a few blocks of text carelessly arranged on a poorly designed GeoCities page. This was back in the early 2000s, I forget exactly when, but the internet was still young and forbidden images of violence and death were like treasures to be sought for some. They certainly were not as commonplace as they are today. I was one such treasure-seeker. I don't know why. I'm squeamish, I probably dislike the sight of blood more than most, but I craved under-standing, and I wanted to see death.

The websites that showed or described death back then would often hide it behind warnings or long essays, explaining why the crime scene photos displayed on their pages were an import-ant educational resource and not at all disrespect-ful or exploitative. The photos themselves would be displayed without commentary, as if the hosts had been rendered speechless by the sight of their own content. Internet speeds were slower so often I would watch as a bloody murder scene was revealed to me one line of pixels at a time. Usually I would then question my motives and scrub the site from my browser history as if doing so would also wipe the memory from my brain. It never did. I can still see them, every one.

Coralie's site was different. There were no pictures on her pages, but the site often came up in my late night searches for the dead because of her vivid descriptions. People would recommend her site in forums and in chatrooms and I must admit I visited several times before I really understood why so many were drawn to her writing. Coralie Westerly saw more beauty in death than in life. In one of her blog posts she wrote, "When we're dead the story is over, and only then does it become art."

I'll tell you what little I know about Coralie from my memory of the brief biography on her site and from snippets I gleamed about her life from our short email exchanges. She was born in Devon in the Southwest of England and spent much of her childhood in the small country village where her parents ran a pub. There are a few stories about her early years scattered among her writings. Most portray nothing particularly unusual, but there are a couple of shocking revelations I'll allow you to discover for yourself. As a teenager, she expressed an interest in medicine and undertook the work required to pursue her chosen career. The work took her to across the Atlantic to the Medical School of the University of Iowa where she transferred after only a year at Cambridge. She wrote openly about her decision to go to Iowa being based purely on them being the first to accept her application. She wanted to leave her birth country by whatever means available for reasons she has not discussed with me or on her blog. After six months of study, she dropped out of Medical School and took a position as a Mortuary Assistant. It was then that she began to write.

Stories the Dead Told Me began as descriptions of the cadavers Coralie worked on as part of her job. Initially, she would write about the physical aspects like their expressions or the clothes that the family had requested she dress them in. Sometimes she would talk about wounds and causes of death, but in a way that never failed to make death seem like an inevitable, perfect ending. She described bruises like flowers and often spoke with resentment about applying make-up to wounds, which she saw as a betrayal of the honest beauty of death. Coralie was fascinated by the way the body changed in death, and I could how that passion had carried her through academia to a point. But it was the fascination of an artist and not a scholar.

In later entries on the blog, Coralie speculated about the people she attended to. She would tell stories about them and how they died. The stories expanded over time and began with the briefest of vignettes, simply detailing their last few hours, days or weeks prior to finding themselves on her table. Later they became epic soliloquies that would sometimes span the entire existence of her subject from birth to death. Coralie would repeat throughout her stories that the dead told her these facts while she prepared their bodies for the casket or the furnace. It was perhaps this repeated insistence that the stories were true that lead to the blog being shut down, because the stories were clearly not true. As you will find out for yourself, the stories were strange indeed.

A few years ago I was working on a film script that included a scene in a mortuary and while researching the location and associated profession to help better picture the scene, I remembered Coralie's blog. I was dismayed to find it no longer existed but after some digging I discovered a Reddit thread from a few years earlier, started by a fellow enthusiast who had also gone looking for the blog and found it missing. The replies were mostly from people like me reminiscing about some of the stories and speculating on what may have happened. One reply stated that Coralie's blog was discovered by her employers who deemed it disrespectful to the families of the dead. While they cited no source, this explanation made sense given that Coralie so clearly loved or at least needed her job so the threat of dismissal may well have prompted her to take the site down. I wonder if it was something smaller though, like a direct email from a concerned family member with enough strong words to prick at her conscience. There were names in the stories and given the content I had always assumed them to be false, Coralie even stated as much in some of the stories, but perhaps this was not the case and I can see why you would not want a loved one to be immortalised on Coralie's blog no matter how well she described their wounds. Perhaps it was something more mundane - a partner who took a dislike to the practice and talked her out of it. Maybe she simply found another hobby.

It was from this Reddit post I did some more investigation on social media and within a few evenings I had an email address. I probably emailed Coralie a dozen times over the course of two years, ranging from a brief 'hello from a fan' to extensive essays about her writing and its impact on me and others. I had suspected the email address was incorrect or no longer active when one day I received a reply.

Coralie was always very brief in her correspondence, but she agreed to send me her stories, each and every one. She gave me permission to reprint them on her behalf and to extend and embellish them as I saw fit. The facts are hers, as are some descriptions. The names have been changed, for reasons detailed above. Where I have added my own words I have attempted to adopt Coralie's narrative voice as much as possible and I don't know that I've always been successful but I tried my best. I offered to make her co-author, but she refused. I'm not sure she would even have agreed to her name being mentioned at all, but she never emailed to confirm. For a while, she would respond to my questions about the stories and even add more detail, but then she stopped replying at all. I haven't heard from her in over a year, which is why I published this first story.

Coralie, if you are reading, I'm sorry.

Chris Regan, July 2021

PROLOGUE

The dead tell me their stories. I will not pretend that's part of the job; I work for a funeral director and I don't mean to imply any connection to clairvoyance or forensic pathology but bodies tell stories regardless of how or why they ended up in front of me. Fat and muscle tell a story, as do fractured bones and ruptured organs and replacement parts. Tattoos tell me almost as much about a person as their scars do, but it's never the story the owner wanted the ink to tell. Hair adds to the tale and teeth can provide insight. A dead tongue can tell me more about its former owner than that same tongue could have told me in life. And the eyes; those dead, dehydrated eyes tell me everything.

One day your body will tell a story too. I hope it's a nice one. I hope you don't find yourself on my table because the stories the dead tell me are never nice. Sometimes I wonder whether I chose the wrong career. Sometimes I think the career chose me.

The story I'm going to tell in this book is about two men, although I'm only looking at one of them right now. I'm not sure where the other one is at this very moment. I suspect he is very sad. The body I'm looking at tells a story about ghosts and demons and old magic. It's also a story about me, because sometimes I like to put myself into the stories too, whether or not I was there. I'm not always sure if it's my choice to do that or if the dead do it for me as a courtesy.

The story begins with Anton. He's a celebrity. You may even have heard of him were I to use his real name. In this story his name is Anton De Vane, a kind of amalgamation of famed Satanist Anton Le Vey, with whom our Anton shares many qualities, and the actor William De Vane, who was in that one film where his hand gets mangled in a garbage disposal unit. I sometimes wonder if the violent films my dad allowed me to watch as a young child influenced my fascination with body parts, but you and I both know that would be far too much of a simplification.

Anton was once a regular guest on a popular ghost-hunting TV show in the mid-2000s, famed for his on-screen charisma and unusually athletic appearance given his interests. He didn't look how people had come to expect your typical paranormal expert to look, and that's what made him stand out. After a falling out with the producers of the show that made his career, Anton struck out on his own. He would soon make his former colleagues regret their refusal to meet his creative demands when their show was cancelled and his soared to new heights. However, some years later the popularity of ghost-hunting TV shows had waned and Anton found himself touring his live show to a dwindling fanbase. The odd TV special surfaced and found some popularity among nostalgia hunters, but mostly Anton's celebrity status was as dead as the ghosts that paved the way for him to begin with. Now, Anton finds himself among his enablers.

As I already mentioned and will probably mention again, I'm not a forensic pathologist but I can say with some certainty that the cause of Anton's death was blunt force trauma to the head. There are contusions all over his body, but the knock on the head was the killer. It caved his skull in, likely causing intracranial hematoma. I may not be in forensics, but I know some of the words. By the time he came to me, a great deal of stitching and stuffing and draining had already been done so you wouldn't know what had killed him at a glance. The head may well look like a map of hastily stitched flesh with the odd, stray bone fragment acting as a landmark, but it does still resemble a head. I doubt it looked much like a head when he was found.

I'm just an assistant so I don't get to do any of the fun stuff yet. I imagine picking the skull fragments from the brain must have been quite satisfying, like plucking feathers. I used to practice on chickens in the village where I grew up. That's too much about me though, we're interested in Anton.

CHAPTER 1

Ladies and Gentlemen

L et's introduce you to Anton properly, shall we? Here he is at one of his live shows. He hasn't been on TV for a couple of years at this point. We're about two months away from his death. It's a small theatre, smaller than he was used to. He'd never done arenas, but he had sold out a couple of West End venues in the past. By this point he was down to local arts centres and the odd seaside playhouse, which is where we find him now. Eastbourne, as you will know by looking at the average age of the audience.

Anton steps out on stage without fanfare, not because he doesn't care but because he likes this stripped down approach to what he does. He thinks it makes his presentation seem more like science. The audience applauds anyway. Anton drops the act enough to allow a small smile, revealing a little of the vain showman he hides behind his concerned scientist persona. He's wearing black, of course. His trademark outfit is a long, leather coat over a neat three-piece suit but with the shirt untucked and the top button undone. It was a look that tried to say cool, sophisticated and intelligent all at the same time and somehow managed to not fully convey any of those things. The suit/ leather combination may have been quirky when he was in his 20s and may have been his signature in his 30s but now in his 40s it looked like he was cosplaying as himself.

Anton stands under the spotlight in the centre of the bare stage and stretches his arms out to the sides in a gesture that is supposed to invite us into his performance but to me always looked a bit too much like an imitation of Jesus on the cross. You can make your own mind up, of course, don't take my word for it.

"How many people here believe in ghosts?" he says with his performing voice, which is markedly different to his TV voice and even more different to his normal voice, as you will later discover, "I mean, really believe in ghosts. Let's have a show of hands. You can be honest, I won't judge you either way."

Do you raise your hand? I'm not raising mine, not because I don't believe in ghosts, I just think it's a very personal question. It's a complicated question too. I've seen things where I work and in other places. I've heard sounds I shouldn't be hearing. Voices, sometimes. Were these things I saw and heard what you might refer to as ghosts? If I choose to believe they were ghosts, then what does that mean for me? What happens the next time I see something out of the ordinary or I hear my name whispered in the dark again? If I believe then I believe. Then there are more questions, like what do the voices in the dark want from me? It's easier to not believe, although I'm not sure I truly believe in my disbelief.

Of course, my belief changed when the ghosts started turning up more regularly, but I'll explain all that to Anton later.

"What about demons? How many of you believe in demons?"

This is easy for me. My hand is not even halfway up. Demons are what TV ghost hunters invent when your usual common or garden ghost cannot maintain the ratings. Demons are what priests invent when the devil becomes too theoretical to have any impact. But everyone loves a good exorcism. They'll show up for that.

Is your hand still in the air for believing in demons or I have talked you out of it? You don't need to worry, you won't be alone. There are more hands up now than there were for ghosts.

Anton counts the hands then nods as if the numbers tally with his as yet unspoken theories. He turns away and takes a couple of paces across the stage, as if considering this new information. It's a rehearsed movement, but he's rehearsed it so often it almost appears natural.

"I've been doing this job for twenty years now," he says as he turns back to address us. "I've been on over four hundred investigations, not including those I took part in before I was on TV. People still ask me that question. Do you believe? 'Be honest,' they'll say like I said to you, 'when the crew has packed up and the cameras have stopped recording do you really believe in ghosts and demons and things that go bump in the night?'"

He pauses here, as if the answer is anything but inevitable.

"'Yes, of course,' I respond. How could I answer any other way and call myself a paranormal investigator? Except I think it's more complicated than that. You have to get into specifics."

And like that, he has my attention. Is this one of his tricks, I wonder? Does he always tell this story knowing there will be those in the audience who also believes the answer is complicated? It doesn't matter now, I'm all in and ready to change my answer depending on whatever he says next.

"What is a ghost?" he says.

It's not rhetorical. He wants answers. It's audience participation. Go on, answer him then. I'm not going to do it, you do it. No really, I've seen this before, someone puts their hand up and says something stupid because they're nervous, I mean it's not them; the situation is engineered to gestate nervousness, and then they'll be picked on for the rest of the show. I'm not doing that. I hate being the centre of attention. You do it. Oh, it's okay, that lady in the front row with the blue hair and tattoo of a cartoon penguin on the back of her neck. She has her hand up now.

"Is it the spirit of a dead person?" she says, like a child in a primary school maths lesson, unsure if they're walking into a trap or not, which is exactly what he wants.

"The spirit of a dead person," says Anton in a way that suggests he's never heard this theory before and he's taking it all in one word at a time, "Do I believe that the dead return as spirits to haunt the living? Yes, because I've communicated with entities that know things only the dead could know. Does that mean they used to be real live people? I can't say for sure and we'll come onto the alternative in a moment. Good. Next answer."

An older lady has her hand up and says with confidence, "An energy powerful enough to move objects around a room."

Anton points at her like she's just cured cancer and yells, "A poltergeist! Yes. Do I believe in poltergeist activity? I've seen it. I love that you called it an energy. I think that's true. Another one, please."

There's no awkward silence this time, but there is a shuffling and murmuring. Everyone likes that the answers are receiving positive responses so now they want to answer too. Watch this, I'm going to blow the previous answers out of the water.

"They're recordings," I say. "Old stone can record images and sounds sometimes."

I don't know if that's true, I just watched an old TV series about it and I want Anton to think I'm clever.

"Ah, stone tape theory. You have done your homework."

Thank you.

"I've seen it," he says as he looks right at me. "I've caught it on camera."

He turns away, does his thinking walk again, leaves the silence as long as he can until it's just about to feel weird and then with perfect timing he turns back and asks, "Okay, so we have some ideas of the forms ghosts or paranormal energy can take. What can it do?"

He waits and eventually a couple of hands are raised. He points at a young man at the back.

"Walk through walls?" he suggests, then he stifles a laugh.

He doesn't laugh at the stupidity of his own suggestion. He's there with his mates and they dared him to ask a stupid question. There's always a few of them at Anton's shows.

"Well," says Anton, looking like he's seriously considering his response, "Yes, if we're talking about energy then certainly physical obstacles would not restrict some forms of energy. What else?"

A woman in the front row has her hand up. She

had her hand up for the first question as well, but it looked like Anton pretended he hadn't seen her. Maybe she's one of those superfans who follows him all over the country, going to every show so he already knows what she's going to say. His eyes pass over her a couple of times, but then finally he points at her.

"They hurt people," says the woman, a hint of sadness in her voice.

Anton nods, slowly, "Yes. Yes, they do."

Anton pauses, maybe for effect, but I actually wonder if there's genuine thought going on here. The woman's question appears to have triggered something.

"I haven't told this story in a while. It was in my book so many of you will know it already but it's important if we are to understand what we're dealing with tonight."

No, that was rehearsed. He always tells this story, but he had me going for a moment there. Maybe he's getting better.

"My first authentic experience of the paranormal happened when I was eight years old. My older brother convinced me to break into an abandoned house in our village. I spent the night there. I wasn't intending to. My brother locked me in one of the rooms and I couldn't get out. He left me there overnight. You could say it was my first investigation."

Anton pauses, allows us to absorb and understand the horror of this act of cruelty and to consider the effect it must have had on a seven-year-old boy.

"There was something in that room with me. I could feel it. And by the time our dad found me, I had the scars to prove it, physical and mental. So, what was it?"

A few hands go up but we're not on the audience participation bit anymore, we're into the monologue. We've pressed 'play' on the video and now it's started and it won't stop until the end.

"What was in that room?"

Do you want the full story? Anton never tells it anymore, I suppose it gets old after you tell it onstage for the thousandth time but it's worth telling you. This is how Anton tells it in his book.

Anton is eight years old. There's a house near to his home. It's an old house, and it looks creepy. One day Anton goes exploring in the house with his older brother. The house is falling apart, garden overgrown. No one has lived there for decades. Squatters have taken residence on and off over the years but they never stay for long. It's not a friendly house. Anton says in his book that just by looking at the house you could tell bad things happened there once. Still, Anton wants to go in.

They break in through the back door where the wooden frame is loose and splintered and offers no resistance. Inside, the house smells of excrement and rotten timber. The windows are boarded up, so it's dark. They can't see what they're stepping on. In Anton's book he talks about his concern that

they could step on the blood or entrails of sacrificed animals, which always seemed like an unnecessary conjecture to me. They venture upstairs.
One window up there hasn't been boarded, so
there's light coming through onto the landing. The
stairs creak. Anton describes the creaking wood as
the protests of the house that doesn't want them
there.

At the top of the stairs, they find a closed door.
After a cursory exploration of the other rooms reveals nothing, they come back to this door. They
try to force it open and after some considerable
effort it moves. The room beyond is black.

Challenged by his brother, Anton enters the
room alone. His brother shuts the door. He hears
his him run downstairs, laughing. Anton isn't
laughing. Anton tries the door, but it's stuck again.
He can't move it on his own. He hears something
move in the room. He can smell it now. He can feel
its hot breath on the back of his neck. Something
sharp touches the flesh on his arm, followed by
more sharp somethings. He screams.

Anton's brother does not return. Eight-year-old
Anton is abandoned in the dark with this creature
he describes as ultimate, final evil. He describes
how the creature plays with him, disappearing
into the darkness for an hour before returning to
scratch Anton's arm or back just when he thinks
he's safe.

Because of a boring family drama I'm not going
to get into here, Anton's brother doesn't return

until the following day. When he does return to set Anton free, his younger brother screams louder than he had when he was first shut in. Anton's parents are there now. They reassure him that there is nothing in the room. All they can see when he opens the door is Anton on the floor by the door. Anton's fingertips were bleeding from scratching at the door to open it from the inside.

Anton comes to recognise the look people give him when he tells the story, so he leaves out the part about the demon. The scratches heal, the fingernails grow back and the story becomes a cruel sibling prank and nothing more. The story in the book was the first time Anton had revealed what had made him scream when the door opened.

The light from outside illuminated the room, and Anton saw the face of the demon.

Then the creature retreated into the shadows as they pulled Anton from the room. After a few weeks of being told the room was empty, he almost came to believe it himself, until he went to bed at night and then in the dark he would see the face again.

"What was in that room?" he repeats. "It leads me back to an earlier question. Do I believe in demons?"

Anton takes off his coat and lays it on the floor next to him. He spreads it out, adjusts the position a little to make sure the coat is in the light.

"Do I believe in demons? I've been attacked on investigations. They've thrown me down stairs.

I've been scratched and burned. I've had thoughts pushed into my head, the most awful, unimaginable things, and when I've tried to push them out I've suffered migraines like you wouldn't believe. I've had entities visit me in my home. I've seen them attack close friends and girlfriends to get to me."

Those of us who have seen Anton more than once know he will never miss an opportunity to mention girlfriends and the threats they have faced. I suspect the principal purpose is to address what used to be constant speculation about his sexuality when he was on TV. It clearly bothered him enough that he brings up his straightness whenever possible in his stage shows. It also deals with his lack of a long-term partner by suggesting anyone who is close to him is a potential target, like he's every Marvel superhero who ever had a love interest. I think coming out would have served him better because the constant references to past lovers is embarrassing now. Then again, he was on TV when homosexuality could break the career of someone famed as much for their looks as their talent and who knows what that does to your sense of identity.

"Yes, I believe in demons," he states, and he lets the statement hang in the air for a moment before he moves on, "It has always been my opinion that investigating demons is so much more important than hunting for ghosts, so that is where I have focused my talents. I don't investigate hauntings.

I'm not the guy with the tape recorder and the night vision camera walking around old houses in the dark and begging for some form of communication. I learned something the rest of the ghost hunting community has been slow to realise. There's a war going on out there in the dark."

Okay, I've never heard him do this bit before. This is glorious nonsense and I love it. Anton has taken off his waistcoat now.

"They're coming for us. They come for us every night, whether we like it or not, and they have to be stopped. I'm not an investigator. I'm not a ghost hunter. I'm a warrior and I'm bringing the fight to them."

With that he rips open his shirt to reveal a huge crucifix tattoo across his torso. And a six-pack. But we're all just looking at the crucifix, right?

"You've seen the show. You know we were achieving fantastic results in the last episodes, before they took us off air."

He's right, the last few episodes of his show are epic. People used to complain about ghost-hunting shows being boring because there's only so many times you can point at a speck of dust on the camera lens and call it an orb. Anton changed all of that. There were pots and pans flying about. He was shoved into a wall. A cameraman fainted and had to be taken to hospital. One of the guest presenters was possessed by a demon and it was all caught on camera. His critics called it a desperate attempt to generate better viewing figures, but

Anton clearly has a more rational explanation.

"It's because I changed my approach. I respect the peaceful dead, but the restless spirits who remain in this world and the malevolent forces who come with them - these creatures don't deserve any such courtesy. I started calling them out, as I intend to do right now. I want to know what they are and why they're here and they will tell me. You will witness many things in this building tonight. You will witness—"

A phone rings. The break in Anton's flow is so jarring everyone feels it. There's no ringtone, just a loud vibration, but we can all hear it. Anton looks furious.

"Whose phone is that?" he demands.

No one raises their hand this time. You can always tell when someone is genuinely angry. I think it's a primitive thing from when we were animals like cats hissing at each other. Anton has gone from zero to eleven in a split second.

"Whose fucking phone is that? Stand up! Stand up if it's your phone."

He's stalking across the stage from left to right and back again, glaring at us, trying to look each of us in the eye one by one. A couple of people laugh, probably because they're uncomfortable or maybe because they think it's part of the show. One look from Anton and they stop laughing so immediately, like someone pressed their 'mute' button.

He's still going, "Stand up you fucking prick. Stand up and take your fucking call. We're about to go into battle, but you stand up and deal with your fucking babysitter or whatever. Fucking come on then! Where is it?"

He's looking right at you now. You don't have a phone, do you? I'm going to have to pretend we're not together if it was yours. I'm probably going to do that anyway, sorry. Oh, hang on, laughing boy at the back with the stupid question about ghosts walking through walls has come to your rescue. He's clearly trying to hold in the giggles, poor lad.

"Do you think this is a joke or something? I know what you thought, there's some fucking dickhead off the telly coming to town, thinks he can see fucking dead people. Should be a right fucking laugh, but yeah, bell me later. I don't give a fuck."

The phone hasn't rung for ages at this point and for a moment it's difficult to remember what he's even talking about. He looks like he's thinking the same thing. Maybe he's even realising he may not get the audience back on side here.

He takes a breath. "Understand, this is a serious business. This is literally, physically and in every way possible a life or death situation. If you thought you were coming to a talk on famous ghost sightings, you were wrong. If you thought I was going to stand up here and play you EVPs and pull out the Ouija board, you need to leave now. We are going to get to the truth tonight. This building, this ancient building, has seen more tragedy and death than we can imagine and that's what they feed on. We're going to call them out and they won't come out nicely. They will come out kicking and screaming. You will see things, you will feel things. I guarantee this room will be almost empty by the time we're done. They can spot the un-believers and they will root you out and make you believe if they don't make you insane first. Let's give them a head-start. If any of you want to leave; if you don't think you can handle this, you stand up and walk out of here right now."

Laughing boy and a couple of his mates stand up and make their way to the exit. Anton seems satisfied with this. The tension in the room dis-sipates slightly as we all consider the possibility that was perhaps simply part of the act. The phone call must be a plant or maybe even played over the PA. The rant, the swearing, all scripted. Bravo, Mr De Vane, I'm impressed. Except now, the phone is ringing again.

"You have got to be fucking kidding me," shouts Anton as he stomps across the stage. "No one is going anywhere until we find that fucking phone. Empty your pockets, right now. All of you. Fucking do it!"

Oh, no. I've just realised whose phone it is. Have you? I can't watch, it's too embarrassing. I'm half-hoping he doesn't realise. In fact, I'm consider-ing confessing to being the owner of the ringing phone just so he doesn't figure it out. Too late.

Anton is looking down at his jacket. He picks it up slowly, his expression a forced neutral. Is it too much to hope that this could yet be part of the act? Maybe it's some elaborate point he's trying to make about ghost hunting theory? No, I saw the expression drop for a moment. He's mortified.

He answers the phone.

"Chloe? It's not a good time … Hold on, say that again?"

Anton drops his jacket and walks slowly backstage. The other audience members turn to each other in confusion, some standing to leave, others determined to get their money's worth even if that means staring at an empty stage for two hours. I wonder what Chloe told him that was so important he felt he had to abandon the show? How about we find out? Come on, we're going backstage.

I'm excited. I've never been backstage at a theatre before. It's smaller than I expected. Anton doesn't really have a dressing room, just a space to the side of the stage with a sofa and a mirror, but then this is a small venue. He's pacing up and down the small space as he talks.

"What's the problem, I thought they signed off on this?" he says, fury rising. "This is on you, Chloe, you fucking told me, you swore to me they signed off on this. If they pull out now we don't have a series."

Do you want to hear the other side of the conversation too? I know I do. Okay, let's hear what Chloe has to say for herself.

"There wasn't anything we could do," says Chloe. "The family always had concerns. I told you that from day one. This was always a possibility."

"Oh, don't give me that shit, they've seen the show. They should know what to expect from me."

"They saw the Treasurer's House footage."

Anton hesitates. "How the fuck did they see that? Don't tell me it's on fucking YouTube again. I told you, I will pay for someone to sit and watch YouTube 24/7 just to make sure no one uploads that video again and you said I was overreacting. Now look what's happened!"

"And I said you'd be better off having it out in the open," argues Chloe, clearly finding herself on a familiar battleground, "Otherwise people hear rumours and they go looking for it and then it's ten times more shocking than they think it's going to be."

Anton takes this in. He sits down on the sofa.

"Fine," he says, "Fuck it. Find me something else. Find me something good, something no one has ever seen before. Something we can build a show out of."

"There's no time," says Chloe. "We were due to shoot tomorrow. We paid all the hire costs, the crew are ready to go. I'll have a look but if you ask me we'd be better going back to somewhere we've done before. We can call the series 'Revisitations' or something, and it's about you going back to your most famous haunts."

"No one gives a fuck," says Anton, defeated.

He hangs up on Chloe and tosses the phone to one side. We are witnessing the failure of Anton

De Vane's last attempt to save his career. His only remaining options now are panto or one of those reality TV shows where he'll have to eat spiders or something. I feel bad for him, don't you? Nice moment for our entrance though. I thought we were going to have to wait backstage with all the other superfans, but Chloe has really given us a rare opportunity here. Are you going to tell him or should I? Fine, I'll do it.

I step into the room, immediately aware I am in a forbidden space; a sentiment confirmed by Anton's stern glare. I'm conscious I only have one shot at this so I get right to the point.

"Mr De Vane," I say and then regret it because I sound like a superfan, "There's a ghost in my house."

I see the rage cross his face for a moment, but when he looks at me, he obviously decides I'm not worth the trouble, and his expression moves easily from anger to boredom.

"Would you like me to sign a book?" he says, "That usually does the trick."

"I'm serious," I persist, and then I realise where I messed up so I correct my opening statement. "There is a demon in my house. I can prove it."

Anton reaches into his pocket and hands me a business card.

"Call that number," he says. "Speak to Chloe, my producer. She'll have one of her interns follow up with you. If it checks out, we'll be there."

All roads lead to Chloe. I want to tell him more

about the things that have been happening in the house. I want to explain the history. I was naïve enough to think he might be interested. No matter, we will speak to this Chloe and we will perform for her underlings and then maybe Anton will come. If not, we'll find someone else.

CHAPTER 2

The Ghost Story

We're in a pub now. I'm in a pub. You're not here with me this time because it's a kind of private meeting. You can sit at the bar and watch what happens from there. It's a small pub and there's no music or anything, it's one of those old-fashioned places with a darts board and a dog. It's not even that busy either. Go on, order whatever you like. I'm afraid this may not be as melodramatic as that last bit, but it would be useful for you to meet the other guy.

You seem a bit confused, but I suppose this is the first time you've really seen what I look like now. We were sitting in the dark before. Yes, I have many tattoos. I'm a tattoo artist. No, I didn't practice on myself, not anywhere visible anyway. I had around fifty of my own before I started tattooing people myself. People always say I'm too young to have this much ink and then they ask stupid questions like, aren't you worried about what they'll look like when you get older? What about when you have a baby? I hate people. I love my tattoos and my artist friends who gave them to me. I'll tell you the stories behind some of them if you like, but it will have to be later because he's here now.

He walks in with a confused look on his face, like someone who has never been in a pub before and isn't even sure he's allowed to be in there, although the beer gut suggests that is not the case. He's wearing a suit, shirt untucked, tie undone, like he's just come from some kind of awful office job, which is exactly where he has come from. When not confused, he has a kind face and would probably resemble a man in his mid-thirties if he didn't have the first signs of grey creeping into his hair and maybe if he lost a little weight. As it is, he looks more like late forties, although I suspect the truth is somewhere between the two.

I don't wave or say anything, even though I know he's looking for me. It's a tactic I read about, like turning up to a meeting late on purpose so you draw all the attention to yourself. In this situation Tom is a few minutes late, I am already here and I have a somewhat elevated status because I have more knowledge than he does. I know the pub that he has walked into for the first time; I know where we'll be sitting because I chose the table, and I know how the conversation is going to go because I called him here for a very specific reason and have some idea of how he is going to respond. Tom has clearly never been here before, doesn't know what I look like or where I'm sitting, and has only a limited understanding of what I'm about to tell him. Oh, I think he's spotted me. He's walking over, still unsure, but then I'm not helping him out at all.

"Coralie?" he intones, as if sounding out my name for the first time.

I'm used to my name being a question.

"Yes?" I could make this so much easier, but I'm enjoying myself now.

"It's Tom. Tom Burgess. We've been emailing?"

Have we? No, that's enough. Let's move things forward.

"Yes, of course. Tom, hi!" I stand up because I'm awful at social interactions and my awkwardness causes me to lose all the status I'd gained by ignoring him.

Tom offers me his hand. I shake it, it's far too formal a greeting, but I like it. Suddenly this feels like a business meeting, which excites me at first but then makes me question why I'm excited as the very thought of a formal business meeting is so dull I can feel my brain cells dying just imagining it, yet somehow a pretend business meeting is different. I keep forgetting I said I was going to be myself this time. I don't think Tom will respond well to a performance but I so enjoy pretending that I find it hard to resist sometimes.

"Can I get you a drink?" he says, looking at my pint of stout on the table in a way that suggests he wants me to say no because he can't really afford to buy a round, which instantly makes me want to take him up on the offer.

"No," I decline, as I pat myself on the back with an invisible hand for behaving myself, "I'm fine. You go ahead."

I sit back down and watch Tom at the bar while I pretend to scribble in my sketchbook. I instantly like him, which I don't do very often. He seems like a nice man, probably too nice if his awkwardness around me is anything to go by, but I like that too because I can relate. I wasn't expecting a nice man because the tone of the email exchange, while not unpleasant, wasn't exactly friendly either. I suspect Tom deals with his fair share of time-wasters and probably assumes the worst. I also assume the worst of people so my wording wasn't the most polite either. I had predicted that either Tom wouldn't show or he would, but he'd be a dick and I'd have to make my excuses and leave. Him being nice is a good sign, although I accept it may make things difficult later on.

Tom carefully places a pint of lager down on the table, then takes off his coat and hangs it over the back of his chair. As he sits down, he accidentally dunks the end of his tie in his beer and as he pulls it out, he looks up to see if I've noticed. I pretend I haven't. As an added diversion from his now half-soaked tie, he draws attention to my sketchbook.

"Are you an artist?" he asks.

I could be rude here. I mean it is a stupid question to ask someone with a sketchbook but I reply, "Tattoos."

He looks at my arms now, like you did, only he smiles when he sees them.

"It must take a steady hand to do that all day," he says, "It's not like you can rub it out if you make a mistake."

"I've had a lot of practice. And made a lot of mistakes but it's been a while since the last one. Do you have any?"

Tom sips his lager, then shakes his head. "No. In my line of work there's something to be said for keeping the flesh pure. Not that I'm against them, not at all. To be honest, I don't think it makes any difference. I just like to present a certain image."

His line of work. Now we're getting to it. This is how I know Tom, in case you were wondering. It's about his job. His pretend job, not his boring paid job but we'll get there, I have questions too.

"Do you do this full time?"

"No," he says with a nervous laugh, "I work in insurance. Investigating doesn't pay very much, not the way I do it."

"What does that mean?"

"It means I won't charge if I find nothing."

"How often do you charge?"

Tom considers this for a moment, perhaps running several draft responses through his head before settling on, "Let's just say I've been working in insurance for a long time. You can make of that what you like. Maybe this thing you want me to do isn't something I'm very good at. But I won't rip you off and I won't lie to you. If I find nothing I'll be honest about it."

I know that already because he states the same things several times over on his website. It comes across like a bit of a gimmick, to be honest; the thing you would expect to see on some kind of online training scam. 'Complete our course in 10 weeks and we guarantee you will have doubled your money or we will refund you in full,' they will say, but the terms and conditions will disagree. Yes, I speak as a victim of one such scam, of which I am not proud but I thought spread betting may have been a viable second income. It was a different time and money is no longer at the top of my list of worries.

"It's not a gimmick," he says when I accuse him of such, "I promise. Few people are honest in this game but I assure you, I am."

Someone saying they're honest is rarely admissible evidence of said honesty but I decide it will have to do and I ask, "So how does this work?"

Tom visibly relaxes, obviously more comfortable with this part of the conversation. "We start with the basics. Why did you call me?"

"My dad died last month," I say, and then I wait for the, 'I'm sorry' but it never comes.

"Then what happened?" Tom prompts.

"He didn't have a will, so it's taken a while to sort out but it looks like I'm going to get the house."

"Do you want the house?"

"I want to sell it. I don't want to live there."

"So, this is about money." Tom looks a little disappointed as he says this.

"It was," I try to be as reassuring in my response as possible, "It's not anymore. I went back to the house for the first time last week. I hadn't been there since ... I don't know. Since I was thirteen."

For the first time in our conversation, that confused look is back on Tom's face that he had when he walked in. I suspect he's had this same conversation many times before where someone inherits their parent's house; they want to sell it but they think it's haunted and then he goes along, proves that it's not and doesn't get paid. That I haven't been to my dad's house since my early teens must deviate from the usual tale.

"Why?" he asks when I don't immediately fill in the backstory.

"I don't know," I say, because I want him to work for it.

"You haven't been to you dad's house since you were a child. There has to be a reason."

"That's not what this is about."

"I don't know that yet. If you ran away from home and that house is the home you ran away from then I think it may be important."

I realise now that I'm not just being difficult

because I'm enjoying myself, but that I really don't want to talk about it. I haven't really talked to anyone about it for a very long time. I know the part I came here to tell him about, I've rehearsed that, but the rest of the story isn't quite ready to be told. I'm going to have to improvise.

"I didn't say I ran away," I stall.

"Did you?"

"I thought this was about the ghosts," moving to dismissal, "I have other problems, I've got fucking loads, but I didn't call you about any of them."

Tom sits back and sips his pint and I realise now that's he's the one running the conversation because he knows where it ends up and not me. I thought I would tell him my ghost story and it would shock him. He would then agree to take on the problem and that would be that. I see now that Tom has his own script for this encounter, and I'm playing my part line by line. More concerning is the realisation that this is not a done deal. I had assumed that the amateur ghost hunter would jump at any chance to test out the equipment they've been buying from eBay, but Tom is clearly more discerning. I've underestimated him.

"It's all connected," says Tom with a fresh confidence. "If you want me to help you, I need you to be honest with me. I need you to tell me everything."

I don't reply right away because I'm not sure how to respond yet. Everything? Could I tell him everything right now? From the beginning? I've told no one the entire story in one sitting. If I reveal anything about my upbringing at all I will usually spread out the revelations over time to optimise pity and even then I don't like to tell one person the whole story. I always liked to think that when I die, which I expect will happen any day now, my acquaintances will meet for drinks after my funeral and will piece together the story of my life from the individual chapters I scattered among them. You lose some of your mystique when you tell someone everything and there is power in mystique. While I'm thinking about this, Tom puts down his pint, still two-thirds full, and stands up.

"Good luck with your ghost, Coralie," he says as he reaches for his coat.

It's perfect. I think I'm in love with him. He had to have rehearsed this moment a million times over because no one does that in real life, but it's worked on me. I'm all in. Tom is my one and only saviour and his way is going to be tough, but it's the only way.

"Tom, wait," I say, and I make sure I'm looking right at him so I catch his little triumphant smirk, which he then tries to hide. "I'll tell you. It's just hard."

Tom sits down again, making a big show of putting his coat back over his chair and making himself comfortable. The eagerness with which he returns to his pint of lager lets him down, though. He was never really going to walk away from that.

"Go on," he says, as he regards his pint, probably considering whether he has time to get another one in, but it's too late now, I've started.

I tell him the story. The full story.

"Dad used to hurt me. Badly. He thought there was something wrong with me and he thought by doing these things to me he could fix it. He wasn't well."

"Did the two of you live alone?" Tom asks.

"No. My mum was there, too. He thought it was her fault. He thought that whatever was wrong with her had gone into me."

"Did he hurt her too?"

"He killed her."

I shouldn't say that. I don't know that it's true. It was worth it for the look of shock on Tom's face. I can see he's trying to hide it; trying to act like this is a story he hears daily. I imagine most of the stories he hears are unimaginative fantasies dreamt up by bored, middle-aged paranormal enthusiasts who consider themselves experts because they've seen every episode of *Ghost Adventures*.

"I think he killed her," I correct myself but the damage is done. "I never really found out what happened. I'd gone by then. I left home when I was thirteen. I ran away, like you said. I thought that whatever might happen to me out on the streets couldn't be any worse than at home. I was mostly right. I got lucky with Jake."

"Boyfriend?" and the way he says this I know he is single and I can tell that it weighs on him and probably affects the way he interacts with women.

I want to say yes, but I tell the truth, "He's my

boss. He took me on as an unofficial apprentice. I think he always wanted kids. He asked no questions, just taught me to ink and now here we are. I hadn't thought about Dad in years, not really. Then I heard he died."

Here's what I think is going on in Tom's head. He's considering my story and taking in all the details. He's using his analytical skills that probably serve him well in his insurance job to look for gaps in the tale or anything he thinks I may have withheld on purpose. He's also actively trying to not think about me being single but he's distracted by thoughts of whether it could work between us, whether he would even want it to work, what that relationship would look like. Could a 40-year-old loss adjuster and hobbyist ghost-hunter date a twenty-year-old tattoo artist? I know this mostly because it's how Jake would behave whenever there were young men in the studio. He'd talk business, but the moment they were gone he'd tell me what he was really thinking. It was never anything sinister, just the desires of a lonely, middle-aged man desperate to believe there was still some chance he could find love and clinging to any possibility that presented itself, no matter how unrealistic. I think that's why I'd warmed to Tom. He reminded me of Jake.

Which is ridiculous because if I stood the two men next to each other they would appear to be visual opposites, the straight, conservative wage slave and the gay punk tattooist who never worked for The Man in his life. As long as they didn't talk about politics or music, they would probably get along. Jake would tell Tom his UFO stories, and Tom would playfully debunk them. Maybe I should set Jake and Tom up? I don't know for a fact that Tom is straight; I mean, he definitely is, but you never know. He might find a kindred spirit in Jake, and I could kind of see it working. Jake needs looking after really and it shouldn't be my job anymore. Now I'm the one fantasising, but Tom still hasn't responded.

Finally, Tom focuses on the question he has been trying to form despite the rollercoaster love story his imagination just took him on. "If you hadn't been in contact with your family for so long, how did you know he was dead?"

"I didn't exactly move very far. The house is in Hove."

I forget, you don't know where I live. Jake's tattoo studio is in the North Laines in Brighton and he lets me stay in the flat above, which is tiny and filthy and nothing works, but it's mine. He used to use it for storage, but he cleared it out for me not long after he found me. Those first few years were weirdly easy. I still went to school and Jake pretended to be my dad if anything ever came up. He told me later he was terrified he'd be found out, and they'd take me away. But no one ever asked. The reality was I was doing better at school than when I was living with Dad, so if any teachers ever had any concerns, they probably decided it was better to leave me be. My attendance was up from zero and I'd stopped turning up covered in bruises, so they left me alone.

Dad's house was maybe a half-hour walk from my new home and the school was in between the two, but I never bumped into him and he certainly never came looking for me. I was terrified he try to would find me at first, then after a few months I resented the fact that he never did. It was around then that I decided he must have killed Mum because she would have come looking. Jake offered to do something about it, but I wouldn't let him. I didn't want Dad to get into trouble.

"Specifically, how did you receive the news?" Tom presses, hung up on what I consider the least interesting part of the story. "Did the hospital contact you? A relative you're still in contact with?"

"An old schoolfriend contacted me through the Instagram page I use for work. Is that specific enough? Why is this important?"

"It's all important," says Tom, and he's back on script, "There are so many factors to consider with a haunting. I need to understand all of them if I'm going to help you."

"Can I get to the part with the ghost?"

Tom doesn't say 'no', he just ignores the question and asks instead, "Do you feel any guilt about what happened to your mum?"

When he says that word, a picture appears. We're in a garden, probably not ours because it's a nice garden, it's most likely a beer garden. The sun is shining and there's this moment of happiness. I think back to it repeatedly. Nothing specific happened, really, but I just knew we were happy.

"She told me to leave," I tell him, "She helped me do it. She packed my bags for me and everything."

"That's not what I asked," Tom says with that glimmer of a smile again because he clearly enjoys this game.

"I know what you asked and I won't answer it," I say, knowing I have to draw a line in the sand here, "That's not what I'm here for."

Tom folds his arms and does his best disappointed teacher look. I wonder how many times he has practiced that look. I suspect he's used to getting his own way in these conversations. He thinks this is one of his skills. People open up to Tom; they tell him their darkest secrets. All he does is listen and leave room for the inevitable confessions. I don't want to play, but he will not let it go.

"There is a reason for my questions, Coralie," he says, attempting to take the tone of a stern mother, presumably because I won't talk about mine, "The more I understand about you the more I can help you. I know this may be difficult. I know we're dealing with a hard time in your past, but I need you to take me there and show me what happened to you. I've been doing these investigations for over twenty years now and I know I'm being forward but if we don't talk about this now, as part of this meeting, then it's likely we never will and I won't be able to help you. I need you to tell me about your mum."

"I don't like talking about her."

"Why? Weren't you close?"

"Yes, we were close." I'm getting angry now and I can feel tears and that makes me more angry because I was supposed to be the one in control here.

"Then what is it?" Tom pushes again. "Why don't you like to talk about her?"

"I can't!" I shout as the tears come, "Not while he's here."

Tom opens his mouth to speak, then stops. I've derailed him again, and he's lost his place in the script. I look for something to dry my eyes with and Tom hands me a handkerchief. I hate him for that because no one carries handkerchiefs around with them anymore, but he does because this is part of his process. His success at making me cry refocuses his attention.

"While who's here?" he asks.

Should we tell him? I wasn't going to, but now I think I have to. I point over to the door where he's been standing the whole time, glaring at us.

"It's my dad."

CHAPTER 3

Hear Nothing See Nothing Say Nothing

The song is by the '80s punk band Discharge. Most of Jake's music was vintage punk, or weird, avant-garde post-punk like The Pop Group. He played it from CDs on an ancient stereo stack that included a double-cassette player and a turntable on the top. It was splattered with flecks of paint from the last time he decorated and sometimes the old CDs would get stuck and he'd have to thump it, but much like his outdated tattoo machines, it worked most of the time and that was all we needed.

All Jake's music choices came with stories. A song would start and he would shout over the opening guitar riff to tell anyone who would listen about the time he was on tour with that band and someone was so drunk or high they did something ridiculous, dangerous and/or illegal but they were on tour and it was a different time so no one cared. I think most of these were stories he had read in the stack of old music magazines he kept in the bathroom and weren't eyewitness accounts, but I never picked him up on it. Sometimes he would tell sad stories about people he used to know who were no longer with us and I could tell these stories were true. Jake hid a vast amount of sadness behind his stories.

Customers would often question how we could concentrate with the music playing so loud, but I'd become so used to it that the idea of working in silence made me uncomfortable. I wasn't sure I could concentrate without the music. The music also drowns out the buzzing of the tattoo gun, which I never minded. But Jake can't stand it. He says it reminds him of being at the dentist. I don't know what happened the last time Jake went to dentist, but one look at his teeth will tell you it was a long time ago and was traumatic enough to guarantee he never went back. That he persisted in the tattoo business despite the constant reminders of painful dental trauma is proof of his commitment to the ink.

The small studio is two rooms and a bathroom next door to a music shop in Brighton's North Laines, where the first hipsters were born. There's a reception area with an old, threadbare sofa and then the studio itself with just enough space for two of us to work, although I hate working with another person in the room. Small-talk with the customer is bad enough but if I have to pretend to be nice to my co-workers as well it makes concentration very difficult. This is another reason I'm thankful for the music and that Jake is going deaf, prematurely perhaps for a man in his early 50s but I suspect it's the decade he spent touring tiny live venues with his old band that has numbed that particular sense. If there is someone else in the poorly ventilated room, it means they too would have a customer so that's four of us in a space that struggles to hold two. For this reason I try to book appointments either first thing in the morning or late in the afternoon, so I have the studio to myself.

I've known Jake long enough that we don't have to attempt small talk if we happen to be working at the same time. Sure, he'll his endless stories but he's given me so much that if all he needs me to do in return is listen I can't argue with that. I'm not so keen on the other artists who work there. Beatrice is a little older than me and started out at an upmarket tattoo place in London that was even on one of those reality shows where they fix people's bad life choices (Bea wasn't a featured artist in the show, she just worked at the studio, but she has very strong opinions on her former colleagues). She's very good at her art and probably better than we deserve, but she wants the authentic Brighton experience and Jake's studio definitely provides that. Cameron is Jake's latest apprentice and one of those frustrating natural talents who seems to be great at everything without ever really trying too hard. Once he came into work drunk after a few lunchtime pints too many and he was supposed to be working on this really intricate portrait of Pinhead from the *Hellraiser* movies on this guy's arm. I tried to talk him out of it. He could barely stand, but he wouldn't listen. The tattoo was incredible, one of the best I've seen. I hate him for that.

I've never found tattooing easy, even after years of practice and mentoring from Jake. I like the sketching part and coming up with designs, but I still find flesh unpredictable and unreliable as a canvas. When I used to practice on Jake, back when he had space between the existing ink to practice on, my hand would shake uncontrollably. He taught me to stop thinking of the flesh as people. This is why I don't enjoy talking to my customers as I work. If you are in my chair, you are a canvas and a canvas doesn't talk. After a while I started applying this logic to people outside the studio as well. Sometimes it helps me make it through the day.

Now we're listening to *Sham 69* and Jake is telling a story about ex-frontman Jimmy Pursey and the time a few years back when he stormed the opening of a new gallery that was showing some of his work and started ripping his own paintings from the walls. Jake's voice was part of the process for me now, like the music, the sound of the tattoo gun, and the seagulls outside the open window.

I'm working on DJ. That's her name, I've never asked why, it's one of those Brighton names that will have an entirely unrelated and nonsensical origin so it's best not to ask. DJ came to me two years ago and requested the biggest piece I'd ever been asked to do. It's a full-body tattoo that runs from the ankle of her left foot and up her leg before winding itself around her waist and ending on her back. The tattoo itself depicts the branches of a tree that transforms as it moves up her body. Sometimes there are flowers growing from the branches and sometimes there are thorns. In the center, in the middle of DJ's back, there is a cage with a peregrine falcon inside (I know, not the type of bird you would usually expect to see in a cage, you can ask DJ to explain and about twenty minutes in you will realise you were okay with not knowing).

I tried to pass DJ to another artist at first. I suggested Jake, but it wasn't really his style and he didn't have the patience for it. There was another artist there at the time, Chelsea, but they had already made plans to move to another studio and left shortly afterwards. It was me or nobody, and I needed the money. Jake told me it would be good to challenge myself, but I'm still not sure I agree. I used to see DJ's tattoo when I closed my eyes at night. Now I have nightmares about it.

DJ would pay me for a couple of hours whenever she saved up the cash. Sometimes she would come in once a week for a month, other times I wouldn't see her for long stretches of time but then just as I would convince myself she was never coming back she'd walk in again. Bit by bit, branch by branch, thorn by thorn, the tattoo took shape. It's nearly finished now and at the point Jake joins in with the chorus to *If The Kids Are United*, I'm adding some last detail to the falcon's eye in the dead centre of DJ's upper back. DJ has long since learned not to talk to me while I'm working. She lies completely still on her front, her arms folded under her chin. If she feels any pain, she has never mentioned it, which I'm grateful for. My gloved hand hovers over the falcon's eye. I want to add more detail because the eye feels important, being at the heart of the entire piece. I add a couple of lines to the iris but I'm nervous about it. The tattoo is so close to being finished but the eye isn't quite right and I know it. DJ hasn't mentioned it and probably should anyone else spot the irregularity they will be too polite to tell her but I will know and I'm aware this is my last opportunity to fix it. It's also my last opportunity to make a mistake.

I place my left hand down just under DJ's shoulder blade to hold my canvas steady, and I move in. The tattoo gun buzzes as the needle hits the flesh. A shadow moves across the doorway and that's when I see Dad standing there watching me. DJ screams. Jake grabs my hand and his expression is a mix of horror and disappointment that I've never seen before. When I look down at DJ's back, what I see makes little sense. It was only a split second. I couldn't have done that. The falcon is ruined. The ultra-thin, miniscule line I was adding to the iris is now a network of jagged lines moving outwards. The lines are everywhere, all over the falcon and the cage and the tree. There's blood too, like I've used the tattoo gun to scratch the lines into the flesh. No wonder she screamed.

Jake ushers me outside and says he will fix it. I know he can't fix the tattoo, it's a mess. This is bad for him. He has an excellent reputation but as one of his favourite sayings goes, 'it takes a lifetime to build up a good rep and one bad tat to lose it'. I'm the bad tattoo. It's my fault but I feel nothing. Dad is still there, and he's smiling now. I think he did it on purpose.

Tom listens as I finish telling the story and then he moves to sip his lager again, but finds his glass empty. He takes out his wallet and starts counting the change.

"It's okay," I say, "I'll get the next round."

As I walk to the bar, I wonder how someone like Tom with a real, grown-up job doesn't have money. Obviously being an honest ghost hunter isn't paying the bills, but I always thought people who wore ties to work made good money. I suspect he spends all his disposable income on ghost hunting equipment, but then there's always the possibility I've read him wrong. Maybe he has a family at home with children and one of those giant trampolines in the garden that I assume the government issue you with once you have kids. I decide I won't ask. It's his business. I order the beers and turn back to Tom, expecting him to be scrolling through something on his phone. That's the rule if you're waiting for someone. You scroll. Tom is flicking through my sketchbook.

"Sorry," he says as I place the drinks down on the table, "I'm fascinated by artists. I was never very good at drawing so it's like magic to me."

"It's okay," I say, although it's not really okay, but the compliment helped balance out my first reaction.

The balance is enough, though. I'm not taking the compliment. I don't deserve compliments on my work after what I did to DJ. My worst work of art is out there in the world, walking around with my moment of madness scratched into her back. I should have been a painter. Painters don't have to worry about bumping into their mistakes in the street.

I sit down, and now Tom takes out his phone and places it on the table.

"Do you mind if I record this?" he asks.

I wonder why he's only decided to record this now, but I suspect he wasn't taking me all that seriously at first. I must have passed his test, but whether it was a test of credibility or curiosity, I'll never know. I nod, anyway. I don't really like being recorded but I trust Tom enough already to believe this will be for personal use and won't end up as part of a podcast or YouTube video. I checked and

Tom didn't appear to have either, which was part of the reason I contacted him over some others I found.

"It's really important you provide me with as much detail as possible," he says, gulping down a more generous measure of lager than he had been doing and I wonder if the recording is to compensate for the effects of alcohol on his analytical skills.

I nod again and Tom asks, "How often do you see him?"

"All the time. He follows me."

"The sighting in the tattoo studio, what time did that take place?"

"I think it was around three in the afternoon."

Tom takes out a notepad and writes this down, which is what I thought the recording was for. I can't tell if he's doubling up on notes for professional reasons or because he's trying to impress me so I'll hire him.

He looks down at the time on his phone.

"It's 8.37 now so there's no apparent correlation between the times," he says, stumbling a little over the word 'correlation,' "Where else have you seen him?"

"In my room. I haven't slept much since this started."

"And when did it start? Was the tattoo studio the first time? Actually, when did that happen, the date I mean?"

"It was last Saturday, so like four days ago. I

started seeing him after I visited the house for the first time a couple of days before that."

"Where exactly in the house was the first sighting?"

It's early morning. I go to the house before work because I want to get it over with and not have it become one of those jobs I keep pushing to the back of my 'To do' list. I picked up the key a week ago and went to the house then but I couldn't do it. Even looking at the house made me feel nauseous, but I felt worse afterwards when I realised I would have to go back. This time I would either push through the nausea or give up entirely.

My Plan B was to ask Jake for help. I thought maybe if he would sort everything and sell it on, he could take a cut of the proceeds. To be honest, he could have taken it all. I didn't care about the money. A week earlier I hadn't even known it was a possibility. I thought I'd erased Dad from my story like a page torn from my sketchbook.

I open the door. It's dark inside. There are no windows in the narrow entrance hall and it's as creepy as I remember it. For a moment I consider calling Jake and asking him to check the house out before I go in. No, I'm being ridiculous. The house is empty. He's gone.

I give the lounge a brief inspection. The solicitors had someone clear the place so there are none of his things here, which is how I wanted it. There's a smell, probably cigarette smoke, but it's been so long I don't even associate that smell with him anymore. The first time Jake smoked in front of me I nearly threw up, but he wasn't going to quit on account of me, so I had to get used to it. It's Jake's smell now, not his.

I hear a sound; the creaking of a floorboard somewhere above. I tell myself it's nothing. Old houses have noises.

The kitchen is a mess. The pots and pans and utensils are gone, but he clearly hadn't cleaned in years. The wall over the hob has a grease overcoat, the floor carpeted in rotten leftovers, stains that dried decades earlier and the odd empty cereal box or milk carton. Some labels on the old packaging look older than I am. When I hear the creaking again, I realise that despite the mess I'd still rather stay in that kitchen than go upstairs.

I turn back to the door for a moment. I imagine myself leaving and walking down the street. I don't even have to be here, do I? Does it matter if the house remains unsold? It could just stay here, empty. Let the squatters have it if they want it.

I make myself do it. I go upstairs.

I check the bathroom first, which on first glance appears more filthy than the kitchen, so I decide not to venture further inside. There's a distinct smell in there and it's not one I recognise, but I don't need to know where it's coming from.

The spare room is next, which used to be my room. There's some old furniture in there and it's blocking the door, so I have to make do with peeking through the gap. I hadn't realised how difficult looking into my old room would be. I knew his room would be hard, but I had an idea my room was okay because I felt some sanctuary in there. Looking through into that room now, I realise I'd imagined that sanctuary after I'd left because it was easier than remembering what really happened. There was no sanctuary in that room and there never had been.

I stay there at the top of the stairs outside the door to my old room for a long time, knowing there's only one room left. His room.

Dad's room was only really a bedroom when we first moved in. When he started having his ideas, he used the bedroom for that and he slept downstairs. He did all kinds of things to that room to make it work. I try to ignore all this when I walk in and I head straight for the window. I decide I just want to check out the state of the garden because you can get an excellent view from up there. I tell myself that this is the only reason I'm going into that room. Then I see a shadow out of the corner of my eye.

"That was when I saw him," I say.

"Is it always like that?" asks Tom. "A shadow in your peripheral vision?"

I'm still in the room and don't hear the question. Dad is right there, looking at me. I don't scream; I don't run, I just stare at him. I don't understand how he's there. I know he's dead. I'm scared he'll try to hurt me, but just like when I was a child, I don't move. I wait for it to happen.

I work out what Tom must have asked and I respond, "Sometimes."

"Do you wear glasses?"

Dad just looks at me. He doesn't move. He's wearing the old grey suit he used to wear every day. He used to work in an office doing something I never understood, local council maybe. One day he stopped working there, but he kept wearing the suit. I can smell that suit as I look at him and I know it's just a memory and not an actual smell, but it's there and it brings more memories with it. It wasn't just cigarettes; it was mould and whiskey and vomit and rot. How could I forget that smell?

"Contacts?" Tom asks again, pointing to his eyes as if miming putting lenses in.

I know where he's going with this and I should appreciate his attention to the facts but I'm still frustrated and I respond, "I don't need fucking glasses, if that's what you're asking. My eyesight is fine."

"Do you want me to fix this or not?" he asks, and it's part of his script again so I know I haven't hurt his feelings but I'm wary of what's coming next.

"I want you to get rid of the ghost of my dead dad, yes."

Tom sits back and I feel another rehearsed monologue is imminent. "What if it turned out there was no ghost? What if we took a trip to the opticians tomorrow and an extra pair of glasses takes care of the shadow? Just hypothetically, no judgment but just imagine that's what happens.

That's what you want, isn't it? That solves your problem, doesn't it?"

I decide to play along. "I thought you were here because you investigate ghosts?"

"I investigate reported paranormal phenomena," is how the monologue begins, "Nine times out of ten what's happening isn't anything paranormal. It's noises caused by bad plumbing, a pigeon trapped in the chimney stack, an undiagnosed health problem. Just last week I went to a house where a woman reported all the cupboards in her kitchen opened by themselves. It took me five minutes and a spirit level to work out there was a subsidence issue. The house was leaning ever so slightly to one side because of ground movement, not a ghost at all."

I know he's fishing for follow-up questions on his example, but I'm bored. I want to skip to the end, so I ask the question he really wants me to ask. "You said nine times out of ten. What about the circumstances that are paranormal?"

"I haven't found any yet."

Tom leaves a dramatic pause here. As much as I find the performance tiresome I appreciate Tom's altruism. If he has truly experienced nothing genuinely unexplainable that means he has never been paid for his work and yes, maybe that just makes him an enthusiastic hobbyist but equally maybe he really cares about the truth. Or perhaps he makes all of this stuff up because he thinks it sounds cool. Actually, I wonder if he just gets his kicks from telling people their ghosts are invented because he seems to be really enjoying himself now.

"I say nine out of ten to give people some hope before revealing that their hauntings are no different from the bog-standard household problems the rest of us are dealing with."

Okay, I wasn't expecting such an honest response so I reply, "You think I want this to be happening to me?"

"Don't you?" he says and before I can stop him, he's off again. "Most people love a good haunting. Even those who claim not to believe in ghosts will encourage a dinner party ghost story. It's exciting, isn't it? The idea of proving the existence of an afterlife is compelling enough but when you go further and it becomes this battle against the forces of darkness within your own living room, who wouldn't want to dine out on a story like that?"

I'm beginning to understand why Tom has never experienced any paranormal activity. I doubt many of his clients progress past the interview stage. I try to disregard the accusation that I'm perhaps making up Dad's ghost for attention. I wish that was the case because then I could go back to my life but it's not and the proof is standing right behind Tom, it's just that he can't see it.

"It's more serious than that," I insist. "I can't work anymore. Jake said I can come back anytime, sure, but how can do that knowing that he'll be there? How can I do anything?"

Then I can't help myself and I ask, "Do you even believe in ghosts?"

"No," he says plainly, "I don't."

And with this I think I'm done.

I don't know how to respond, but Tom fills the silence for me with the answer to a question I haven't asked. "I like solving problems. You have a problem, I would like to solve it."

"Can you recommend anyone else?" I ask, annoyed at the desperation I can hear in my voice. "Someone who actually believes in the problem I want fixing?"

Tom goes into another speech. "There is no shortage of ghost hunters online. They'll come to your house, they'll set up night vision cameras and whip out their bullshit EVP recorders and they'll tell you they are going to put the spirits to rest. The truth is, they're not interested in helping you, they just want evidence of your ghost. They'll see the light catch a speck of dust on their camera lens and they'll declare it to be the most intense haunting they've ever experienced. Their 'spirit boxes' will catch half-a-second of Radio 1 and they'll extrapolate an entire saga about the family that used to live in your house and how they all died mysteriously and now they want you to die too, but burning some sage will probably fix it. They'll take what they can get and then leave you to deal with the consequences. If you wanted to contact one of those ghost hunters, they're easy enough to find.

You contacted me. My website makes my method and my belief or lack thereof quite clear. You called me because you, like me, care about the truth."

It's actually a pretty good speech, it's just that the last part isn't true and I tell him, "You were the first result that came up. I was looking for someone local and I want this sorted as soon as. I can't book an appointment for three weeks from now. I'm planning on leaving the country, going travelling, but I don't want him to come with me. If you think you can figure this out, then let's do it. You don't have to tell me why you're doing it or what you think I'm experiencing. Just tell me when you can start and let's go."

"Even if the end result isn't what you think it is?"

I gather my things to make it clear the meeting is over. "I just need it sorted. Can you start tomorrow?"

"I only do this on weekends."

The facade drops and Tom is back to being a loss adjuster who chases ghosts in his spare time.

"Tomorrow. You have the address. I'll pay you whatever, even if it turns out I just need glasses."

I put on my coat and head for the door, leaving Tom to finish his beer. Dad doesn't follow me out, which makes a change. When I leave, he's standing over Tom, looking down at him. Maybe he wants Tom to accept the truth, too.

CHAPTER 4

In My House There's A Place I Can Hide

Here I am. I came back. You didn't think I would, but I'm here and I'm going to put things right. You're going to be right here with me.

The main bedroom is the largest room in the house and takes up most of the upper floor. I don't know if they built it that way. It seems odd exploring the house now with its cramped kitchen and lounge downstairs and a room twice the size upstairs. I'm not even sure it makes mathematical sense, but then I've never measured it. The surveyor's report suggested nothing anomalous. Maybe it's just that this room feels bigger to me because what happened in here changed everything.

I take my time to look around, knowing help is on the way. The room is as bare as I remember it. Dad stripped the wallpaper and carpets when I still lived here. There's a cheap, peeling laminate flooring covering the floorboards, which I suspect he put down to cover up what he used to do in here. The bed has gone, which I'm thankful for. There's a single, naked lightbulb hanging from the ceiling. The bulb flickers every now and again as if struggling to hold on to its light. I switch it off. It's morning and though the grime on the windows keeps out most of the sun, there's enough light to see.

I never did get to see the garden on my last visit, so I try to shift some of the grime with my sleeve. I don't know how the windows came to be so dirty, but the substance on the surface is greasy and black. I wonder if Dad did it on purpose to keep people from seeing in. I mostly spread it around but manage to clear away a small patch so I can look down into the jungle below. In the years I lived here, I don't think I ever saw Dad working on the garden and it showed. The small fenced-off space is mostly grass and bushes and a few broken household items like an old fridge and a TV. The mattress is down there too.

It looks like Dad tried to hide it, but I can see the corner of the mattress peeking out from under a pile of old chairs and other rubbish. I recognise the stains. I thought I'd relived all the terrible memories the house was going to give me, but seeing the mattress brings back more. I don't want to remember but they're coming thick and fast, the screaming and the pain and the awful things my dad did.

Do you hear that? There's a shuffling sound. A tapping, even. Is that you? Oh no, it's creaking now. Probably just the floorboards. Whatever it was, I'm grateful for the distraction.

I look over at Dad. I didn't see him at all last night, but he was here, waiting for me. He's standing in the corner of the room now, watching. I can't read his expression, it's strangely neutral like he hasn't decided how to feel about this yet. I hope he doesn't like it once we get started. I hope this hurts him. He never wanted anyone to know what happened here. That was why he started locking me in my room so I wouldn't go out and tell people like I had that day at school.

There was a bruise on my arm and one of my teachers, Mr Ball, asked about it. He was one of the mean ones usually, so the sudden concern in his eyes as he looked at me derailed my stock response. I forgot what I was supposed to say, and I told him I fell down the stairs, which was worse because that's the kind of thing people say when they're covering up abuse. Dad had told me to say I got into a fight with neighbour's kids because it's both specific enough to stop them checking and also vague enough to cut off any follow-up questions. Mr Ball didn't believe my story about the stairs and called my dad to check. He didn't tell him what I'd said, he just asked what had happened and Dad went into the story about the neighbours, which made things worse. Dad had to come into school for a meeting. It was the only day he changed his suit. He made sure I was more careful after that.

A knock at the door. He's here. You wait, I'll get the door. Won't be a minute.

I run downstairs and open the front door. There he is, looking up at the house. I suspect he's trying to work out how it will look into the promos. There's a van parked on the road outside. Parking is restricted here, but before I can say anything, he shoves past me to get into the house and I decide not to tell him. He's like one of those Hollywood producers you used to hear about eyeing up his latest starlet on the casting couch except it's not me on the couch, it's the house. He only has eyes for the house. Maybe that's how it should be, but it still makes me feel cheap and a little used.

He barely looks at the kitchen and lounge, instead heading for the stairs. He walks into the room and stands in the dead centre. He turns slowly, looking at each wall and then at the ceiling.

"This is where you saw him," says Anton.

It's a statement, not a question, but I nod anyway. I know I told him it was this room, but he's performing, presumably just for us. We should feel privileged.

"It's smaller than I thought it would be," he says, and now he's the condescending TV producer again.

"Is that a problem?" I ask because I'm not really

sure whether it was an observation or an accusation.

He shakes his head. "No, not at all. It's claustrophobic, I like it. Just thinking about the cameras."

I don't respond to this. Cameras aren't my problem.

Anton takes a deep breath, back in character. He closes his eyes. I look over at Dad and he's smiling again now. I can't stand to look at that smile. He has these thin lips, and he lost most of his teeth so his smile is this narrow, black gash across his face, like he's been cut open with a scalpel but instead of blood, I can just see darkness inside him. This isn't a new thing, he always looked like that. Again, maybe I'm exaggerating. Dad smiling always meant he'd had an idea, and that usually meant something bad was about to happen.

Anton hasn't seen Dad. Part of me hoped he would have given all the things he claimed to have seen on his TV show, usually when the cameras weren't rolling. I think I knew he wasn't really going to see him, though. That would be too easy.

"Should I leave the room?" I ask, partly to remind him I'm still standing here.

Anton shakes his head but says nothing. Then he raises his hand slowly and points to the door in the corner of the room. He opens his eyes, looks at the door, and then at me.

"Where does that doorway lead?" he asks.

I suppose I forgot to mention the doorway. I suppose I had deliberately been trying not to look at it. I suppose I thought maybe if I didn't look at it I'd forget where it went and what was on the other side.

"Up to the loft," I say.

"What's in the loft?"

"No idea," I tell him, "I can't find the key to the door."

The part about the key is true. I don't know where it is and I don't want to know. I don't even know if the door is actually locked, it's just wishful thinking. Anton walks over, gives it a tug. It doesn't move, so at least we won't be going up there anytime soon. The lie was the part about not knowing what's up there. I know. We both do, don't we?

"Unusual, isn't it?" Anton says, "A house this size I'd expect a hatch in the ceiling, not a doorway with its own stairs. I assume there are stairs?"

I nod.

"Very odd," he continues. "There must be another room up there. What was it used for?"

"I was never allowed to go up," I lie again.

"Interesting. We'll need to find that key."

I suspect this may have gone on longer, but I'm saved further interrogation by the sound of a plate smashing downstairs in the kitchen.

"That's just the crew setting up," Anton explains. "They can be clumsy."

"What are they doing in the kitchen?"

"They're establishing a nerve centre."

I almost laugh at this. There's something absurd in the idea of Dad's grubby little kitchen being referred to as nerve centre.

"It's where they'll monitor the cameras," Anton offers by way of a further explanation, and then he follows this up with, "You have watched the show, haven't you?"

This is most definitely an accusation. I wonder what he will do if I tell him I haven't. Will he walk out? Probably not. It will more likely give him a free pass to tell me stories about past adventures at any available opportunity. Still, I need to keep track of my lies so I'm better off going with the truth about something so trivial.

"Yes, I've seen it," I confirm without detailing the full extent of my research into Anton's techniques.

"Here's how this works," he starts. "They'll be setting up a series of remote cameras around the house. Given the atmosphere in this room, I'm going to suggest four in here, one on the landing and a couple downstairs, just in case. The nerve centre is where we monitor the feeds and—"

He stops mid-sentence then looks at me with wide eyes and a "Shh!"

I wasn't speaking so I just look at him. He's looking up at the ceiling. The creaking again, although it sounds different. I'd maybe call it more of a rumble.

"It's an old house," I tell him.

"I've been in houses much older than this and pipes don't make sounds like that."

Anton appears to be in danger of neglecting the purpose of his visit, so I remind him, "It's not the noises that bother me. It's the ghost."

I look over at Dad when I say this, but Anton doesn't notice. He's looking up at the ceiling with a mix of concern and concentration on his face. I wonder how many hours of practice in front of the mirror were spent perfecting that look. I see now he makes his eyes do most of the heavy lifting while the rest of his face remains neutral, so he seems aloof whilst also conveying emotion. He turns those eyes on me now.

"Talk to me," he commands.

"I told your producer everything," I say, which is an exaggeration but I really don't want to tell the story again.

"You did, and Chloe put it all into a neat, bullet-pointed email for me, but I need more than that. I want you to look me in the eyes and tell me what you have experienced in this house."

I take a breath, and then I begin. "This used to be my parents' bedroom. I remember jumping up and down on their bed when I was a child. I forget how old I was, maybe four?"

"I don't need your entire life story," Anton cuts me off and steps closer.

"You asked for my experiences in this house."

"The paranormal experiences," closer still as I try to remember if I closed the door behind me, "The reason I'm here."

I don't like this game and I want to shut it down

so I try, "If you didn't already know what's been happening to me you wouldn't be here."

"I need to hear it from you." he takes another step.

I can smell his breath now. It's minty. He knew he would do this and took precautions. He places his hands firmly on my shoulders and bends down slightly so his eyes are level with mine.

"Coralie, you mustn't fight me on this," he says as his eyes go to work again. "They will try to use you to stop me. They will get inside your head. They will make you hate me. You must put that aside. If we're going to get you through this, we must do it together."

I feel like I recognise the speech from a Hammer horror film, but I play along.

"It's my dad," I confess. "I saw him in this room. After he died."

"I'm sorry for your loss," says Anton, releasing his grip on my shoulders.

He's forgotten I'd already told him about Dad dying. If his producer had gone to the trouble of summarising my story, he hadn't read it. He doesn't care.

Anton steps away, looking at the room again, then he asks, "Did he die in here?"

I don't want to tell him. I knew he'd be like this and I know it's all a performance, but I still expected him to do some research or something. I thought he would pretend to care; I thought that was part of his act. I try telling myself it doesn't really matter, but I'm hurt.

"Did your father die in this room?" Anton demands.

"Yes," I say finally, remembering why we are all here, "Yes, he did."

"Good."

"What the fuck?" and this time I mostly force the anger as I'm finding his absence of sympathy amusing.

"I'm sorry," says Anton with sad eyes and a forced compassion in his voice, "I know how that sounded, but if he died in this room, it means his spirit will be stronger here. We have a very good chance of being able to communicate with him, which means we have an even better chance at sending him on his way. Were you with him at the end?"

I hesitate here because I want him to think this is difficult for me. I want him to think he's risking my trust and compliance by asking such personal questions. I also hesitate because I'm about to lie in front of my dad.

"Yes," I say when I can feel the silence becoming awkward, "I was. I'd been staying here since he first became ill. On the night he died I heard him struggling to breathe, so I came into his room and I found him. I called an ambulance, but it was too late. I did everything..."

I even choke back some tears here. I can feel Dad standing closer to me now. I will not look at him, but his movement suggests I provoked a reaction.

Good.

"You tried to save him," says Anton, sad eyes working overtime, "That's important, Coralie. We can use that. Were the two of you close?"

Now I really can't look at Dad because I'm worried I'll laugh.

"He was my dad," I say, to close off any further questions of this nature.

It's not good enough for Anton though, who continues, "Coralie, if you want me to help you and your dad you have to let me in. Did you and your father have a close relationship?"

I have to be careful here but I have put some thought into how I will answer this question. It has to be something heartfelt but generic; something that sounds like I mean it but doesn't lend itself to further questioning. I need a story to throw him off the scent. What do fathers and daughters normally do together? I need something specific enough to be believable but vague enough to cut off any follow-up, like Dad taught me. I can feel the weight of the silence since he asked, so I decide I will just have to say the next thing that comes into my head.

"He was my best friend."

Dad hasn't made a sound since I first saw him after his death and I'm not even sure it's possible for him to produce sounds, but I could swear I heard him cough when I say this. I'm probably imagining it.

Anton steps forward again and gives me an

awkward hug. I can't tell if this is because he believed me or because we're both following a script and in the stage directions it says, "They hug." It doesn't feel improvised. I stand rigid and whether he realises he has overstepped or not, the moment is over quickly and he backs away again.

"We're going to help him," he says, "I promise you."

I make the mistake of turning around and I see Dad. It's impossible not to. His face is up against mine. He's angry, and it's like the fury has distorted his features somehow. The anger has caused vibrations to ripple through his form and he's losing his shape. His eyes are larger, almost pushing themselves out of his skull, and the mouth is wide and open in a roar. The distorted expression is so strong I can feel his anger like a physical force, faint, but it's there. I look at Anton to see if he's noticed it, too.

"Coralie, what's wrong?" he asks, with what almost seems like sincerity.

Go on, say it. Tell me I look like I've seen a ghost.

He doesn't say it, he just looks around the room as if the finale of his favourite TV show is playing somewhere and he can't see the TV. Finally, seeing nothing, he turns to me again and I just catch a glimpse of his frustration before he switches back to concern.

"He didn't like that," I tell him.

"What do you mean?" asks Anton, moving closer again.

"My dad. He doesn't like it when people touch me."

This isn't what Dad didn't like at all, and I can feel his fury growing from a light vibration to a weak breeze. This time I'm sure Anton feels it too because he steps back. I think for a moment he might be afraid.

He looks around the room again, then he asks, "How do you know he doesn't like it?"

With perfect timing, there is a loud knock. Anton looks at me and yes, there is genuine terror in his eyes now.

"There's someone at the door," I tell him, "I'll just be a minute."

"I'll come with you," he says without hesitation. "I should see how the crew are getting along."

I leave the room slowly and Anton almost pushes past me in his desperation to not be left alone in there. I don't know if I'm disappointed he's afraid because I thought he'd be braver or happy because it's the reaction I wanted. I know I'm relieved to see him feel something real, at least. He should be afraid. We're dealing with an angry ghost now.

Downstairs the house is all noise and activity. It's a small crew of four. The producer is Chloe, we've heard about her already. She's talking on her mobile, demanding things I don't understand. I don't like her. She's overdressed for my dad's house, looking like she's attending a business meeting in the City rather than a ghost investigation. I don't think she appears on camera, so I'm not sure who she's trying to impress. I wonder if it's just her uniform.

The rest of the crew is hard at work turning my kitchen into a "nerve centre". There are monitors and laptops and cables everywhere. They ignore me as they work, but they ignore Anton as well, which is more surprising. I know he probably greeted them outside already, maybe a few of them shared a taxi, but I'd at least expect some questions from them on the room or on how set-up is going. He strides past them and they don't even look at him.

I'm at the front door now. Anton is still behind me, possibly looking to get out of the house for some air or possibly for good. When I open the door, I feel him stop in his tracks, and I look back at him for his reaction. The colour has drained from his face and he seems more shocked than he did in the room. Should I say it? I really want to, but I don't think I'd be able to keep a straight face.

Tom looks at Anton. He tries to hide his shock at seeing TV's Anton de Vane in person, but his face betrays him.

"Oh, fuck." he says.

This should be interesting.

CHAPTER 5

The Reunion

"Hello, Tom," says Anton, "It's been a while."

Tom won't look at Anton and instead looks at me and says, "You should've told me. I can't do this with him here."

"I need all the help I can get," I say, and then I add, "You told me you don't believe in ghosts."

"He doesn't," Anton joins, "And he can be rather evangelical about his non-belief, bordering on aggressive. He's not going to help you."

"I didn't realise you two knew each other?" I say.

It's true, I didn't. I should have been a bit more thorough in my research. I thought they were in different leagues, Anton the celebrity ghost hunter and Tom the enthusiastic hobbyist. I hadn't really expected Anton to take me seriously even when Chloe confirmed a date with me over email; she had prefaced her confirmation with a disclaimer that it depended on Anton's agreement. I thought Anton didn't do the small hauntings like mine anymore, even with his career in decline. I suppose I should have warned Anton that I had contacted another ghost hunter, but I don't think it would have made any difference. I also wasn't entirely convinced Tom was going to show up, either. I certainly hadn't anticipated how wonderfully awkward a moment it would be when they realised they would both be investigating the same haunting. If you were to remove the supernatural element and compare this to another typical household problem, a leaking tap for example, then I can see that hiring two plumbers to deal with the same job at the same time would seem quite ridiculous. My problem is not of the typical household variety though and I can't help feeling that perhaps their differing stances on their chosen areas of expertise may even be of some considerable benefit.

"Oh, we know each other," says Anton, "Tom here has been trolling me for years."

Tom doesn't go for Anton's bait because I think he's wondering whether to just walk away. In the perfect, excruciating silence that follows, I look at Anton and then back at Tom, and I understand. When Anton says trolling I assume he means Tom has been leaving negative comments on his content. I can see how that might work. Anton has clips from his shows online and they're usually the big moments - being pushed down a flight of stairs, being hit by a rock thrown from nowhere, even the time he was apparently possessed by a demonic entity. I can imagine Tom spending his evenings typing furious essays in the comments section under the videos to debunk someone more successful than he is. I can see that if Tom truly believes that proof of the paranormal is as scarce as he makes out, then seeing someone profit from the opposite position must be frustrating. I can also see that of all the things he expected to have to do today, confronting his nemesis in the flesh probably wasn't one of them.

When I sense Tom is about to move I try to rescue the situation with, "I actually think you might balance each other out."

"That's not really how this works," Anton responds without hesitation. "Belief is incredibly important with something like this. How are we supposed to cleanse your house of spirits if every time they react you have this guy telling you it's just down to creaky floorboards and old pipes?"

"I'm sorry, Coralie," says Tom, perhaps inevitably, "I can't help you."

Tom turns and walks away down the road, his backpack bouncing up and down as he walks, making him look like a schoolkid having a tantrum. It's his decision. I could leave him to it, but I've already decided I don't like Anton very much and between the two I'd much rather have Tom. I'm kind of hoping that if I can convince Tom to come back, then Anton will leave. I follow him down the road.

"Let him go," Anton advises, "We need to get started."

"Start without me!" I shout back over my shoulder.

Tom is walking away at speed, and I have to break into a run to catch up with him.

"Tom, wait!" I say as I reach out to touch his shoulder.

He turns and I see tears in his eyes. This is not what I was expecting.

"You should've told me," he says again, intending to scream at me, but his voice breaks up as the words come out.

"I'm sorry," I say. "I didn't think he was going to show up. I didn't think you were going to show up. You didn't seem interested."

"He does this every time," Tom says, drying his eyes on his sleeve, "Every time I get a lead he shows up and takes it out from under me."

In his book, Anton talks about how he picked up his first TV ghost hunting job via an audition and it was his appearance on that show that gave him his career. I wonder if Tom auditioned that day, too. By the way Tom has reacted I suspect he did. From then on, his nemesis in the field would always be the first to investigate high profile haunts and would forever leave Tom on the outside. There was a time when Tom might have been able to find work as a skeptic, but then those roles all went to university professors and authors in the field, not part-time ghost hunters who had to work their hobby around their insurance job.

"Just come back," I suggest. "I want you there. You can keep Anton in check."

"He won't let me," he says in a way that suggests he knows Anton really won't concede.

I wonder if there's some sort of restraining order in place.

I try something else. "How about you come back tomorrow? You can do your investigation then and we can compare notes with what Anton turned up."

I immediately regret saying this because I want the problem solved today. Then again, if Anton can't fix it I do like the idea of having a back-up.

Tom isn't listening. He's staring at the house. I wait a moment in case this is him changing his mind, but I think he's just waiting for me to give up. So I do.

"It was nice meeting you, Tom," I say, and then I walk back to the house.

It's his decision, and as much as I think it might be easier with him, I doubt that there is any way he will help me with Dad. I suspect he would simply conclude that yes; I do need glasses, but he was nice to me and didn't lie as much as Anton, so I'm sad to see him go.

"You should've told me he was coming," says Anton, then he looks down at the monitor in the newly established 'nerve centre'.

I was hoping for more of a reaction than that. Anton put on an unfamiliar face for Tom, which means he let his performance for me slip ever so slightly. I thought he'd be angry about that. I'd like to see some anger from him now, wouldn't you? He's playing a combination of professional and showman but I'd like to see the angry Anton we saw on stage. He'll need that anger if he's going to deal with Dad.

I move into the lounge, suddenly feeling unwelcome in my own home. But then that's an odd thought because it hasn't been my home for a while. There's a woman unpacking a camera and I give myself a telling off for initially assuming she was the make-up person.

"Are we ready to set up the cameras?" she shouts over to Anton.

"I don't know, Beth," he says, appearing in the doorway behind me, "What do you think, Coralie? Do you still want my help or would you rather your story be dismissed as sounds and shadows? Tom is local, isn't he? It would be no trouble to get him back."

I'm impressed that he went with snark rather than anger but I'm also irritated by his tone. I feel like calling his bluff and telling him to leave because I'd rather have Tom's help.

"I'm sorry," I say, although I'm not sorry at all but I'm assuming this is what he wants from me, "I don't know how this works, I thought having more people here would help."

"We're not moving house here, Coralie. We're exorcising the spirits of the dead. You don't need an army of wannabe ghost hunters to do that. Not when you have me."

I see now there was no danger of him leaving, he just wanted to do the speech and fair enough, it's a good line. He probably paid writers to come up with that.

"Go ahead," I say, "Do your thing."

Anton smiles and nods to Beth. She rolls her eyes then hauls the heavy camera case towards the stairs. One of the two men in the kitchen opens up a large make-up kit on the counter and begins setting up his materials. The other man, who I assume is in charge of sound given the microphones he is checking, is the first of the crew to look up and acknowledge my presence.

"I'm Coralie," I announce, realising no one else is going to introduce me.

"Steve," says the guy with the microphones.

Of course the sound man is called Steve. I probably could have guessed that.

Steve nods towards the rapidly expanding make-up department that is now taking over the whole counter and says, "That's Lee."

"Morning," says Lee without turning to look at me.

"Beth is our one woman camera department," he continues, "But don't call her that. We used to be able to afford a whole team but these days we're working on a fraction of the budget, which she hates and she also hates that she can't afford not to take the work."

I nod, trying to take in this sudden flood of information about people I've only just met.

"And you know Chloe."

Chloe says nothing in response, her phone apparently glued to the side of her face, although she doesn't appear to be talking to anyone.

"Thanks. Nice to meet you all," I say, feeling the conversation already becoming stilted and awkward.

I wish I didn't have to be here for this. When you call a tradesperson to work on your house, you can leave and expect the work to be done when you get back. Why can't I do that here? I know exactly why, I just wish there was another way. You know how much I hate meeting new people.

"Sorry about all this," says Steve, showing the NASA Control Center that used to be dad's kitchen, "We'll put everything back as it was when we're done."

"It's okay," I shrug, "It's not really my kitchen."

Steve is refreshingly scruffy compared to Anton, Chloe and Lee who all look prepped for the perfect selfie at any moment. He has a long beard that makes him look older than he probably is and his longish hair is a mess. He has a tattoo on his forearm and as soon as I see it, I know he's one of my people. The tattoo looks like a primitive cave painting of a creature.

"That's interesting," I say, pointing at the ink.

"What is it?"

"Oh, it's ridiculous. Hey, you're a tattoo artist, right? I've been thinking of getting it changed into something else."

"Why? I like it."

"But you can't tell what it is."

I shake my head, "Go on, tell me."

Steve stops what he's doing and says, "Okay, so I used to be really into old horror movies, like the Universal ones, you know?"

I nod. Jake loves those films. If we were in the studio with no clients, he'd pull out his old TV and show us films on VHS. I offered to buy him a Blu-ray player once, but he turned me down because he'd just have to buy his entire collection again. It's part of his thing. At home he mostly watches obscure anime that he downloads from various illicit sources on the internet, but in work he likes to pretend he's some kind of relic from a forgotten age of VHS tapes and cassettes. I think he thinks he's staying ahead of the hipster curve. I don't mind. I like those old films.

"I was obsessed with them as a teenager," Steve continues, "I used draw the monsters all the time and then I started drawing them in different styles. I had this idea of doing them as cave paintings, you know, because all the stories come from folklore and stuff so it would make sense if there were cave paintings of like Dracula and the Mummy, but not like they are in the films, they're like prehistoric versions. I built up this whole mythology, and I started writing stories about ancient man fending off these weird creatures we know from movies. The gill man from *Creature from the Black Lagoon* was always my favourite, I think because he fits the whole idea best, he's like basically a dinosaur. That's why I got him as my first tattoo."

I looked again. I could see it now. It was *The Creature from the Black Lagoon* as a cave painting.

"That's really cool," I say, and somehow the first genuine thing I've said all day comes out sounding the most insincere.

"If by cool you mean the nerdiest thing you've ever heard, plus the longest ever explanation for a tattoo."

"Oh, I've heard longer stories," I reassure him, and he smiles.

I think I've found an ally in Steve. It relaxes me a little knowing he'll be here, listening in at least. I hope he gets out of here okay.

"Steve!" shouts Anton from upstairs. "We're ready for the mics!"

"Sorry, duty calls," says Steve, and he picks up a bunch of sound equipment to take upstairs.

"Can I help?" I try, but he's already gone.

I linger in the kitchen a while longer. Lee is still busying himself with his kit. I get the impression he doesn't want to chat, but I also don't really want to go back upstairs just yet.

"Would you like a tea or coffee?" I ask.

"I'm fine, thanks," says Lee.

I start the kettle boiling anyway because I feel like I have to do something. I'll make drinks for everyone. I'll pretend I'm a runner on the crew and not the reason they're here. This is feeling like a bigger undertaking than I imagined, and I'm regretting contacting Anton now. I don't like the way he looks at me, like he's auditioning me; considering whether I'm camera ready. I can see Lee looking at me like that, too. I knew being on camera would be a possibility and I'd told myself I was okay with it if that's what it took to take care of Dad, but now faced with the reality of it, I'm not so sure. I'm wishing Tom was still here.

CHAPTER 6

Showtime

It's mid afternoon now and we're still not ready to start. I've done six rounds of teas and coffees. Chloe ordered in lunch for everyone. I sat on my own in the lounge while the others ate sandwiches upstairs, working as they ate. Steve occasionally popped his head round the door to check I was okay. I am okay. They're keeping Dad occupied so I'm fine. When I last left the room, he was glaring at Anton with that death stare of his, and I was grateful not to be his primary focus for a moment. The only problem is the longer the day goes on, the closer we move towards the moment I'm dreading. I feel like I'm at school waiting for the bus to take us to swimming lessons. I hated swimming lessons, mostly I hated the whole changing room experience, but I wasn't good in the water and the lessons themselves just felt like a regular reminder of my ineptitude. I used to tell myself it wouldn't happen that day, like maybe the bus would break down or maybe the swimming pool would be closed and we wouldn't have to go, which would only make the inevitable arrival of the bus feel even more crushing. I have that same feeling now when Chloe walks into the room.

"We're ready," she says with no hint of enthusiasm or reassurance.

I'm sure Chloe is very good at her job, but surely making your host feel comfortable is part of that job, isn't it? I didn't think it was possible to feel more unwelcome in this house than when I first stepped into Dad's room and saw him there. But Chloe has beaten that. I follow her upstairs, the sound of her heels clacking against the bare floorboards drowning out all other noise. When I step into the room it is almost unrecognizable, adorned with lights and wires and cameras and equipment. It looks like a set, not that I've been on any sets, but it somehow doesn't feel real anymore; it feels like they built this room for us to use today and I'm just a player in the performance, which I suppose is true, really. I like this feeling.

I catch how it looks on Beth's monitor and am impressed to see that she's framed it in a way that reveals none of the technology, so as far as the camera is concerned it's the same old bare room. Anton is standing in the centre, perfectly lit and unmoving. Lee attacks me with powder while Chloe distracts me from the assault.

"We're doing the intro first," she explains, "While we've got the sunlight."

I look over to the window to see that somehow they've cleared the grime off completely.

"Anton will ask you some questions and you just tell him the same story you told me," she continues. "We may run through it a couple of times to make sure we get the best take. Then you'll take him on a house tour so we can see the other rooms. After that we'll lock the place down for the evening."

She says some more stuff and I nod in the right places, but I don't really care anymore. I really want to get this over with now. When you have a leaking tap you aren't really interested in how the plumber is going to stop it, you just want it to stop, right? Maybe that's just me. Maybe I should stop using the leaking tap analogy because the more time I spend with Anton and his crew the less this feels like a standard household maintenance situation.

Lee steps back, looks at my face, then does something with a brush that I don't really see. He gives Chloe a look, which I assume means he's done with me because she then leads me into the centre of the room. Steve walks over with a clip mic and a battery.

"Right," he says, "I need to get you mic'd up. We've not quite upgraded to wireless yet."

He looks embarrassed. This is usually one of those situations when I would enjoy making things as difficult as possible, but I like Steve, so I decide to go easy on him. I take the clip mic and feed it up through my shirt, then pass it to him to find somewhere to put it. He leans in close to clip it to the top of my shirt and I pick up a hint of weed on his breath beneath the minty gum he's used to disguise it. I wonder if there will be some kind of wrap party afterwards and I can hang out with Steve, talking about microphones and cave painting tattoos. He passes the battery pack to me and I clip it onto my belt. The moment is over far too soon and Lee is in my face again with his brush and his powder.

"All good?" asks Anton.

Lee nods.

Steve puts on his headphones and looks at me.

"Testing?" I say.

He gives Anton a thumbs up.

Beth lightly takes my arm and manoeuvres me over to Anton. I want to like Beth as well but similar to Lee and Chloe; I don't think she sees me as a person, just a prop she needs to ensure is lit properly. Maybe that's how you have to be to work in TV or maybe that's what the job does to you. Maybe they'll warm up to me as the day goes on and when Steve invites them for a drink with us, they'll all come along. Lee will act like he's always been my best friend and later, when he goes to the loo or to get a drink, I'll tell Steve he was cold with me in the morning and Steve will nod and say he's always like that and Beth will agree even though she knows she's just as bad. They're good people really, but they don't particularly like working for Anton. All of them had more prestigious TV jobs before, but for a variety of reasons, Anton is currently their best hope of continued employment so they have to put up with him. I'm surprised because I assumed they work for Anton out of an insatiable curiosity about the paranormal. They laugh at this because they didn't believe any of it until today.

I'm speculating. I've no idea why they work for Anton. Maybe he's really nice once you get to know him? I glance over at Dad to see what he makes of all this, but I can't see him. He must be in the shadows somewhere, but the lights are too bright.

"We'll pick up the full introduction downstairs where there's more natural light," says Chloe and for a moment I think she's talking to me but no, she's looking at Anton, "Skip to the house tour."

Anton nods and then asks everyone else in the room if they're ready except me. Beth and Steve give the thumbs up again and we're off.

"So, this is the room where your father passed away," Anton states, getting right into it.

He stares at me and I realise it was a question and not a statement so I reply, "Yes, this was his room."

"What have you experienced in this room since his passing?"

I hesitate again because I'm not sure where to

start, but in the end I don't have to answer at all.

There is a tapping noise from somewhere above. It's quiet, there's barely any sound at all, but Anton heard it. His head snaps up as he gazes at the ceiling. He flings out his arm, open palm to the camera in a dramatic motion intended to quiet the crew, although no one is making any noise.

"It's starting," he says.

I'm surprised he didn't go with something more dramatic like, "And so it begins," but then I think he's aiming for a balance of melodrama and realism. This must be the line he walks all the time when he's on an investigation. Maybe he's better at his job than I thought he was, it's just that his job isn't hunting ghosts, it's making everyone else believe he's hunting ghosts and making them care.

I look up at the ceiling too, so maybe his act is working on me after all. Everyone in the room does. There are cracks in the plasterwork. I wonder about asbestos. I think that if Tom were here, he would say that now. He would recommend I have the ceiling tested for asbestos because maybe I'm suffering from asbestos poisoning and that's why I keep seeing my dead dad everywhere. Case closed. Maybe it's better he's not here.

"Hello?" Anton says. "Is there someone here with us?"

Yes, I want to say, my dad's here. I don't have to say that though because there is another tap-tap-tap from above, louder this time.

"Did you hear that?" Anton is suddenly very excited, "Instant response! We're in for a good show here. It's ready to communicate."

Anton looks over at Chloe. "I need you down in the nerve centre, right now."

It's really hard to keep a straight face when he says 'nerve centre' like that, but I notice no one else is laughing. I suppose you get used to it. Chloe glances down at the schedule on her tablet, clearly irritated that we are already deviating from the plan, but Anton snatches it from her hand.

"Fuck the schedule, we've got audible communication in here! Go!"

Chloe walks to the stairs, entirely unperturbed by Anton's outburst. I'm beginning to understand why she's so unhappy.

"Beth, I want all cameras recording like we're locked down. Same goes for sound. We're doing this now."

Beth and Steve both leap into action, adjusting the various cameras and mics they've rigged around the room. Lee watches for a moment, then saunters to the stairs when he realises his services are not required.

Anton turns me to face him and says, "Once we begin, there's no going back. Whatever or whoever is haunting this house may not mean you any harm at this point but in my experience the spirits of the dead do not react well to being evicted."

I nod and Anton carries on. "The important thing is that we finish. I swear to you I will not leave this house until I'm satisfied it's clear, but you must agree to do the same. Are you ready for this?"

I nod again, but it's obviously not convincing enough because he's holding both my arms now and almost shaking me. "Be certain! Are you prepared to see this through to the end, no matter what happens?"

"Yes," I say, frustrated that I'm submitting to his condescension but equally unwilling to drag this out.

"Okay," he says, "Let's see if we can find out who we're talking to."

Anton steps away and back into the centre of the room again. He looks at Beth and Steve and they both give him a nod. He takes a deep breath then spreads his arms wide at waist height in what I suppose is a welcoming gesture, but like everything Anton does it looks performative and disingenuous.

"I, Anton de Vane, address the spirits who linger this house."

I'm annoyed at the use of the plural here. How many times do I have to tell him that it's just the one spirit? Maybe he's just being thorough, but it seems to me to be further evidence that Anton has not listened to a word I've said.

"Can you hear and understand my voice?" he continues, "Tap once for 'yes' and two for 'no'."

There is a long pause. Anton doesn't move, his arms remaining outstretched like he's frozen in place. Beth and Steve are silent and still, but they must have been through this a thousand times by now. The whole thing suddenly strikes me as ridiculous and I think I'm going to ruin it all by laughing aloud, but then I see Dad staring at me from across the room and it's not funny anymore. Dad doesn't think so, anyway. I think this is really getting to him.

Then, a single tap.

"They're responsive," says Anton, excited again, "That's good. What's your father's name?"

I'm looking right at Dad and he's not moved an inch so I tell Anton, "It wasn't him."

Anton grabs my shoulders again and it almost provokes a physical reaction this time. I'm not tall and being manhandled is number one in my list of irritating things people do. I let this one pass, but next time I'm going to have to put a stop to it.

"Your father's name," he demands, "Quickly!"

"James," I say as slowly as I can, "James Westerly."

Anton releases me and turns his attention back to the ceiling.

"Am I addressing James Westerly?"

There is a long silence. Then another single tap.

"It's him," says Anton. "It's your father."

It's not him. I'm looking right at my father and he's not lifted a finger. I consider telling Anton this, but then I wonder what good it will do. I asked Anton to come here to escalate the situation like he always did in his show. I wanted him to force a reaction. Maybe this is how he does it, by getting things wrong. It could be a great dramatic moment later when he realises his mistake. I understand now that my revelation came too early but I can picture Anton on his knees later, screaming at the ceiling, "The tapping wasn't him!"

I decide to play along.

"Ask him what he wants," I say, knowing I can ask myself, but I've decided to not only play along but to add in a little naivety for good measure.

"You can talk to him yourself," is Anton's predictable response. "He's your dad. Talk to him as if you can see him right here in front of you."

I don't know if it's luck, or it's because he can sense something in the room, but when Anton suggests visualizing my dad he points to the exact spot where Dad is in fact standing. I look at Dad. Dad doesn't look at me, he's focused on Anton now.

"Why are you here?" I ask, trying to disguise the resignation in my voice because I know he's not going to answer me. I've been through this with him many times before now.

We stand in silence for a moment, then Anton says, "A couple of points to consider. Address him as 'Dad', or whatever you used to call him. They like to be reminded of who they were. Second, remember he can only answer 'yes' or 'no'. 'Why' isn't going to produce a response. Think of it like two prisoners tapping on a radiator to communicate between their jail cells."

This strikes me as a weird and unnecessary analogy. Anton is not doing a great job of convincing me of his expertise and yet everything he says is presented with this irritating confidence. I remind myself I've decided to play along, and I do. I think of the kinds of questions people pose to ghosts on TV ghost hunting shows.

"Dad... Are you trapped here?"

Nothing.

"Is something preventing you from leaving?"

This time there is a tap in response but it overlaps my question so I'm unsure whether it's a response to the first question or the latter. Anton is dying to jump in and say something, so I decide to beat him to it and ask the next question that comes into my head.

"Are you alone?"

Anton nods his approval at this one.

Silence again. I wait longer this time and perhaps overstepping my boundaries I even raise a hand to shush Anton when he opens his mouth to interject. He smiles though, so maybe it was part of his plan all along.

There is a single tap and I almost ask my follow-up question, but then there is another tap. No, he is not alone. The ghost of my dad is still staring at Anton. He certainly appears to be alone, but whatever I've been communicating with is saying it is not.

I turn to Anton and ask, "What does that mean?"

Anton thinks for a moment and then asks, "Why did you ask that question about something preventing him from leaving?"

Oh, I wasn't expecting that. I can't tell him it's because it's a thing people say on ghost hunting shows. I decide to make something up.

"It's just something I'd been thinking about," I begin, my mind throwing a story down in front of me like putting down a railway track in front of a rapidly moving train, "He was in so much pain towards the end. I can't figure out why he'd want to come back unless he's unable to leave."

Anton nods, although I'm not sure he understands human emotions.

"Ask him if they want to hurt you," he says.

"Who?" I ask, confused.

"The other spirits. They must be keeping him here for a reason."

I keep forgetting Anton can't see my dad, especially after he pointed him out to me. Anton has a different story in his mind, where Dad is up in the loft with other ghosts. Maybe there's some truth in part of that. We'll find out later.

"Dad?" I ask, addressing the ghost of my father again. "Do the other spirits want to hurt me?"

Silence, although Anton doesn't wait as long as we had been waiting, so I suspect this is the outcome he wanted.

"He's gone," he says.

He's not gone. Dad is right there in front of me. I walk over to him, seeing my chance to prove his existence fading away. I'm not interested in taps from above. I just want to them to see the ghost of my dad like I do. I'm not even interesting in getting rid of him right now, I just want the others to see.

"Dad!" I scream in his face. "Answer me! Am I in danger?"

It's the question Anton wanted me to ask, but I want to know the answer from my father. Am I in danger from him?

"It's no use," says Anton, "They're holding him back. I can feel it."

No, I'm not going along with this anymore and I say, "He's still here."

"Trust me on this, Coralie," says Anton, and I know that if I hadn't crossed to the other side of the room, his hands would be on my shoulders again, "These other, malevolent spirits are the ones we really need to worry about. They will not be happy with him communicating with us like that. We're dealing with demons here, I can feel it."

He's telling a story. He decided on this story before we even started trying to commune with the dead. He probably decided on it before he even met me. I understand now that this is how his process works. Anton works out the events in advance. His skill is not in detecting spirits but in convincing others that the spirits are there so he can tell the best story for his audience. I won't let him get away with this.

"I can see him."

Anton looks at me, confused. I've gone off-script. It's telling that he looks over at Beth for validation I just said what he thought I said before he looks around the room in case he's missed something. I don't think he even believes in ghosts. I think the idea that there could be a genuine spirit in this room is impossible for him and his reaction shows it.

"I know he's still here because he's standing right in front of me," I say, and this time I point to the spot where Dad is still standing.

Anton drops his entire act for a moment and responds like a very normal, very confused person, "There's no one there."

"I know you can't see him, but I'm telling you, I can," I insist.

"How long has he been there?" he asks.

"Since I moved back into this house. Pretty much since the day he died."

"Why didn't you tell me?" he asks, sounding angry and a little accusatory.

"I told you I saw the ghost of my dead dad."

"I believed you saw him once. A one-off. These things usually are," he's back in performance mode, but now he's a university lecturer, "Physical manifestations are rare, almost unheard of in genuine paranormal cases."

He emphasises the word 'genuine' and I spit back, "What's that supposed to mean?"

"Did you tell Chloe about this?" accusing again, although I'm not sure what I've done wrong.

"Yes! Did she tell you? I think she probably did, but you weren't listening," I'm imagining him on the phone to Chloe, pushing her to get to the point as she tries to save his career, "You have no idea what my story is, you just turned up like it was just another episode of your show."

"That's what it is, darling."

The 'darling' part stings like he intended it to. It's what showbiz people say to non-showbiz people to clarify that they're in a different league, living different lives, breathing rarefied air. How can I possibly understand his process when I'm a mere mortal in the presence of a god?

"No, it's not, *darling*," I say, instantly wishing I'd thought of a wittier comeback.

"You're not special, Coralie," he says, growing more angry with every word, "I've been doing this for a long time. This is just another day at work for me. I didn't look into your story because it will be the same story I've heard hundreds of times before in every old, dark house I've ever investigated. I can say with one hundred percent certainty that you did not tell anyone on my crew about what you could see because if you had I wouldn't be here."

So that's it. He thinks I've wasted his time. "You don't believe me," I state.

"People don't see ghosts," he says, "They see shadows. They hear sounds. They feel a presence in the room. What you're talking about, seeing the face of a dead man right in front of you, that's not supernatural. That's something else."

He doesn't elaborate on what the something else is, but the implication is clear enough. For Anton, a haunting must have to fall between two extremes. Obviously if it's just the odd tapping noise or bad feeling, then that's not enough but what I hadn't realised is that it's possible to go too far. The suggestion of an actual ghost I can see all the time is at the opposite extreme and it's pushing believability. Tom thought the same, although he at least believed I had a problem, even if that problem was of my making.

I say nothing else. I just look at Anton and wait for him to finish his diagnosis. While I'm waiting, something catches my attention outside the window. I think there's something moving out there, down in the overgrown garden. I look over my shoulder, but I can't see it now, and Anton is talking again.

"I can't have someone declare with complete certainty that they can see a ghost with their own eyes when the camera doesn't pick up a thing, it just doesn't work like that."

"You know he's here," I say, because part of me still believes that perhaps Anton isn't a complete fraud and has some of the affinity for spirit detection that he claims to have.

Anton mistakenly thinks I'm referring to the tapping he was having a conversation with and says, "It's an old house."

That hurt.

He turns his back on me and walks to the door. I notice that Beth and Steve are still in position and have made no attempt to pack up their equipment or even to question whether they should pack up.

They are still recording, which forces me to consider the possibility that Anton is still performing. He stops at the door and turns to face me once more.

"You're lying to me, aren't you?" he says.

I'm confused. I don't know where he's going with this. He wanted a ghost, and I gave him one, but it wasn't the one he wanted, so now he's trying to push me into confessing something. Confess what? I feel like an actor who has forgotten their lines on stage. I even look to Steve for a prompt, but he is busy monitoring his levels, or he knows exactly what is happening and finds it too awkward to watch. Anton is still looking at me, waiting for an answer. Dad is standing next to him and he's looking at me too now.

"I wish I was lying," I say, honestly.

"Stop!" Anton shouts with a posh schoolteacher voice. "I came here to help you. We will find whatever is in this house. You don't need to lie about seeing a ghost. I told you from the beginning, I need you to be completely honest with me."

He stops, looking over at Beth, which I notice he does a lot, suggesting perhaps she has more power in the team dynamic than her silence lets on. I wonder if he's thinking he's gone a bit too far and wants some sign from Beth on whether he should push further or rein it in. Like Steve, she is busying herself with her camera and won't look Anton in the eye. Then I see it, a slight movement of her hand, but I'm sure it was a thumbs up.

Anton takes a step towards me and says, "Tell me you're lying and I'll stay. I won't judge you. I understand how these experiences can affect our state of mind, but I can't help you if you won't tell me the truth. Tell me it was a lie and we can get back to fixing this."

"I don't understand," I say, and it's true, "Is this the wrong type of haunting for you? I'm looking at my dead dad right now. What is it about this that doesn't work for your show?"

"There's nothing fucking there! Seeing dead people is something that happens in movies, not in real life. You're taking the piss and making me look like a fucking idiot!"

Beth looks up at him now, showing he really has gone too far. When Anton takes a couple more steps towards me, Steve actually moves to intercept. Anton sees this and stops, grabbing the air in front of him as if he's squeezing my shoulders again.

"Tell me it was a lie!" he screams.

That's when Tom runs into the room and shouts, "Everyone out! Now!"

CHAPTER 7

Ritualist

It's been at least four hours since Tom walked away from my father's house after declaring he couldn't be on an investigation with Anton de Vane. Now here he is in Dad's room, looking dishevelled and sweaty. He's wearing the same thick coat he had on when he arrived and with his backpack strapped to his back he looks more like he's heading out on a country walk than a ghost hunt. I also notice mud on his shoes and on his hands along with a couple of dried leaves in his hair that confirm to me that the movement I saw in the garden was Tom. To anyone who hasn't put that together this muddy, sweaty, frantic man must look a little alarming.

"What are you doing here?" asks Anton,

strangely calm in his reaction.

I suppose Anton had set his rage to 11 when he was screaming at me and there's nowhere else to go from there so he's had to dial it down to respond to Tom's sudden appearance. I thought he'd be even more angry given that Tom has presumably ruined his monologue, but maybe it isn't a performance after all and he can react like a human being. For my part, I'm relieved to see Tom. I was feeling the day may have been a waste of everyone's time, but now here's someone who will at least listen to me when I tell him I'm looking at my dad. Dad doesn't seem to have noticed Tom, he's still glaring at Anton. I don't think he likes Anton very much, which is understandable.

"There isn't time to explain," says Tom, frantic "You all have to leave this house immediately."

"Have you completely lost it?" asks Anton. "You can't come onto my location and tell me to leave."

Anton referring to Dad's house as his location visibly angers Dad almost as much as it angers me. I understand his attitude now. As far as Anton is concerned, he hasn't come to my property to investigate my haunting. I've come to him to bear witness to his miracle.

"You are leaving this house, even if I have to drag you all out!" shouts Tom.

When we first met, I couldn't imagine Tom being angry. He didn't seem like a person who would ever be angry about anything, and I certainly could never have imagined him shouting like he is now. He steps towards Anton, his hands raised and I see for the first time that it's not just mud on his fingers, there is a bit of red too. This is exciting. I look over at Steve, hoping to find someone to revel in the excitement with me, but he actually looks rather furious, which is a shame.

"You realise you're on camera. If you touch me..." Anton stops, looking at Tom's hand, "What have you done to your hand? Is that blood?"

"I think you should go," Steve interjects, in a mildly threatening tone unlikely to produce a calm response.

He steps in between Anton and Tom; I presume being the alpha male on set this is what he does whether it's protecting Anton or protecting others from Anton. I thought maybe he'd quite enjoy the idea of his boss being punched in the face by a raving lunatic, but apparently not. I'm disappointed. I look to Beth in case I have a hidden ally there, but Beth looks frightened. I suppose because I sort of know Tom and don't find him at all threatening I have no expectation that this conflict will escalate any further but I can see that to an outside observer it would appear dangerous and on the edge of violence. Realising this I understand why Anton isn't phased because while it may not be a ghost he will have a good YouTube clip on his hands.

"It's okay, Steve," says Anton. "I know him, he's not here to hurt anyone. Why don't you and Beth break for lunch. We'll reset, pick it up again in the afternoon."

Beth emerges from behind her camera and practically sprints for the stairs.

Steve looks at me, then back at Anton. "Are you sure you're okay?"

Anton nods.

Steve looks at me, "You can come too."

I almost laugh in his face, but I try to look like I'm trying to be brave and I shake my head with what I hope looks like forced stoicism.

Steve looks back at Tom and Anton one last time, then follows Beth downstairs.

Tom is still standing with his arms up, palms out as if he's going to do something, but he hasn't decided what yet.

"Anton," Tom starts, calmer now, "You have to listen to me. If we don't get out of here now—"

I'm annoyed at being left out of the equation so I say, "It's my house. I'm not leaving either. Not without an explanation."

"I will explain," says Tom, "But not in here. Believe me, there's no time."

"What's happened, Tom?" Anton asks, softening his tone considerably. "Have you seen something?"

I'm surprised by the concern in Anton's voice and even more by what sounds like a note of compassion in there. I wish I could say I thought it was another performance, but even if I did, I don't know why he would put on an act for Tom.

Tom finally seems to accept that shouting at us to leave is getting him nowhere. He takes a breath, lowers his arms, and addresses Anton.

"There's too much. Something bad is going to happen in this house. It's already started."

I can't help myself so I interject, "I thought you didn't believe in any of this stuff?"

"I don't," he says again, "I have a million explanations for what I just saw but if I'm wrong..."

"So tell us what you saw," Anton commands.

"You won't believe me. Just take my word for it. We'll know one way or another soon enough. If nothing happens, and it probably won't, I'll go on my merry way without a second thought. If I'm right, and what I think is happening is really happening, we're not leaving this house alive. No one is."

Anton looks down at Tom's hands, and I look too. He's trembling.

"You're really scared," says Anton, more to himself than to me or Tom.

"Tom, please," I try, "If it's that important you have to talk to us."

Tom looks at me and hesitates for a moment, then he asks, "Your father, what does he look like?"

"I have a photo..."

Tom shakes his head. "No, I'm forgetting the process. I need to tell you. He's my height. Thin. I'd say he's mid-sixties, maybe older. His hair is mostly grey but with a hint of red remaining. He's clean-shaven. He's wearing a grey suit."

Anton says nothing, but he turns to look at me for confirmation.

"You've seen him," I say.

"When you left me earlier, I looked back at the house and I saw someone standing in the alley that leads to the garden. The man I just described. I thought he must be on the crew. I was so angry I didn't think about it, I just went home."

"People don't see ghosts, Tom," Anton says, not as angry as he was when he told me the same thing, "You know that as well as I do. A physical manifestation is almost always imagined. Like you say, you probably saw someone from the crew going outside for a smoke and because Coralie had told you about her father—"

"I never described him," I interject, "I never said what he was wearing."

"I was on the bus," Tom continues as if he'd never been interrupted, "On the top deck and I thought it was empty but when I stood to leave there he was. He was on the bus. I turned to walk down the steps and he was sitting on the back seat. He was looking at me."

I look at Anton, waiting for his response, but it never comes.

"I decided it couldn't have been him," Tom goes on, "I went to my flat and I unlocked the door and there he was again, sitting on my sofa. He didn't look at me, he was just staring straight ahead. I didn't know what to do. I just stood in the doorway, looking at the back of his head. I stood there for ages. It must have been a good twenty minutes. I blinked, I pinched myself, I did all the stupid cliche things people tell me they do when they see something paranormal. He was still there."

"Tom, you can't expect me to believe…"

Anton trails off when he meets Tom's eyes. I don't need to be looking at Tom to know he is deadly serious.

"I waited," Tom says, "I walked out of the door, back out onto the street, down to the end of the road and then back to my flat. He was still there, on my sofa with his back to me. Then I saw his reflection on the TV screen and I saw his expression. In the reflection, his eyes were on me and he was angry. Then he must have realised I'd seen his face, because he smiled. He smiled, and it was like his face split open from ear to ear. I've never seen anything like it."

Anton looks at Tom and then at me and he says, "You're in on this together, aren't you?"

Tom shakes his head. "I swear Anton, I don't know what it was, but I saw it."

I point at Dad and I ask, "Can you see him now?"

Tom doesn't look at first, but then slowly he turns his head and scans the room.

"No, not in here."

"My dad's ghost is standing right there looking at us!"

Tom shakes his head. "I'm not sure what I saw was a ghost. There are so many possibilities."

"Like what?" I ask, seeing my one chance at being believed fading from view.

"I need to confirm that he's really dead, for a

start," says Tom.

"Are you joking? I buried him."

"Please, Coralie, don't take this personally. I hadn't looked into any of this, but there has to be some kind of explanation. Maybe a relative who looks similar?"

"What about you, Tom?" asks Anton. "Do you still have trouble sleeping? Are you fit and healthy right now?"

"I've considered that possibility too and no, if you must know, I haven't been sleeping well recently."

"Then that's it," Anton declares. "This is exactly why you were never very good at this, Tom, you're too suggestible; too easily influenced. I'm guessing she told you she can see her dad and I can just imagine how you reacted. I suspect you saw a shadow outside the house, a stranger on the bus and then you open the door and who knows what was on your sofa, maybe a pile of clothes but I doubt very much it was the spirit of her dead father."

"What if he saw my dad?" I ask Anton, "Why aren't you prepared to consider that?"

"Are you prepared to consider that?" Anton asks Tom.

"I wasn't," says Tom, "I dismissed it. I left the flat, went for a walk. I had some breakfast, came back and this time he was gone."

"Sleep deprivation exacerbated by hunger plus whatever medication you're on these days," says Anton, "Case closed."

"I thought you were supposed to believe," I say, for my part not quite believing what I'm hearing, "He's the skeptic, not you."

"I believe in paranormal phenomena," Anton argues, echoing something Tom said last night. "Things that are unexplained. I don't believe in the recently deceased walking around in broad daylight."

I think I'm beginning to understand. Jake did an online course on running a small business once and for weeks he was rambling about branding and making sure you have a good USP. Anton has to sell himself as a product so he has to be clear on his USP, which for him is that he investigates paranormal phenomena and more recently demons but the ghosts of the dead aren't something he is particularly interested in, especially not if they're walking around.

"There's something else," says Tom.

Anton looks at him, waiting for him to continue.

"I decided to come back. I've been doing some research into the house and I thought maybe it would be useful for the investigation. I felt bad about storming off this morning."

"Yes, it was rather childish," Anton adds and if I could stand to be close to him, I would have elbowed him in the ribs.

"I saw a shadow in the alley," Tom continues, "This time it was just a shadow. I wanted to check it out to confirm the specifics. I was so relieved not to see him there again."

"That's why you really came back, isn't it?" I say.

Tom nods and continues, "I wanted to convince myself I'd imagined it. I followed the alley into the garden, hoping to see a tree or something moving in the wind and casting a shadow. Have you been there recently? Out in the garden?"

"No," I reply, "It's a mess. Dad just left it to grow."

"There's a pile of junk in one corner, over by the fence," says Tom. "It must've been a compost heap once, but now it's covered in broken furniture and old magazines. There was something sticking out at the bottom. It looked like part of an animal."

"What kind of animal?" asks Anton, and I see that he's hanging on every word of Tom's story now, as am I.

Tom reaches into his pocket. "I knew you wouldn't believe me so…"

He throws something at Anton. His reflexes make him catch it but his revulsion when he sees what it is forces him to drop it immediately. I look at the small, white shape on the floor. It's the head of a bird.

"Is that a chicken's head?" Anton asks, his disgust clear from his voice.

"It's the head of a white hen," says Tom.

Anton looks at the head then turns to me, "Did your dad keep chickens?"

I shake my head. Tom is taking something else out of his pocket and this time he places it carefully on the same floorboard as the hen's head. This one is similarly mutilated but I can see that the feathers are black and the red stuff isn't blood, it's solid and fleshy.

"A rooster?" I say, realising I've walked into playing Tom's game here, but I'm engaged now.

"A black rooster," says Tom, then he looks at Anton as if he's expecting a response.

The three of us look down at the two decapitated heads in silence for a moment. I don't know what to make of this. Dad didn't like animals, but I couldn't see him going to the trouble of obtaining two birds in order to mutilate them. There was the possibility that they belonged to a neighbour and perhaps they'd been annoying Dad, so he'd disposed of them. But again it was a bit of a stretch. The house was an end terrace, so there was only one neighbour and their garden was more overgrown and cluttered than ours.

"Maybe a fox got to them," says Anton, still running with the theory that my dad kept these animals in the garden, which he didn't.

"A white hen and a black rooster," Tom addresses Anton like I'm not in the room. "They've been sacrificed. You know what that means."

"It means you have too much time on your hands if you expect me to believe this."

"A black rooster and a white hen," Tom says again, as if reversing the order will make Anton understand, "Do you know what the date is today?"

Enough, I think and I say, "Can one of you please tell me what the fuck is going on?"

Tom looks at me now and becomes almost accusatory as he says, "These birds were killed recently. Are you really telling me you know nothing about this?"

I don't know what's happening. I brought these men here to help me. Neither of them believe I'm being haunted. Now both of them are looking at me like I'm the fraud. After both of them did their little performances for me, now they dare to look at me like I'm the one pretending. They think I'm making this up, and now I have to defend myself while the ghost of my dead dad watches from the corner of the room. I don't even know where to start. The dead birds mean nothing to me, but I don't know how to convince them of that.

"I told you, I've barely been here," I say, hoping this will bring an end to the interrogation.

"The blood was still wet," says Tom, "This can't have happened more than an hour ago."

Now I'm really at a loss. How can they possibly think I had something to do with this? An hour ago? I was here. Wouldn't we have heard two birds being decapitated an hour ago? Steve has basically wired the house for sound, wouldn't he have picked something up? I'm so flustered and confused I can't get any of these arguments from my brain to my mouth.

"Is there something you need to tell us?" says Anton, now fully onside with the man he dismissed as an internet troll a few short hours ago.

"You're taking his side now?" and I know I sound pathetic but I can't quite believe this is happening.

"You say you see dead people right in front of you and there are two sacrificed birds in your back garden," Anton continues, as if I should immediately see the connection.

"Why are they sacrificed and not just dead?" and now I'm the one with the rational analysis, "I told you my dad didn't keep chickens but I don't know, maybe he did. I definitely don't know what happened to them. I don't get why this is such a big deal."

Anton looks at me, staring into my eyes and I stare back, determined not to look away because I know if I do he'll take that as confirmation I'm lying about all of this.

"It's part of a ritual," Anton finally explains and I think he would have detailed the whole thing if only because he enjoys the sound of his own voice but Tom cuts him off.

"She knows what it means."

"What ritual?" I ask, and I'm only addressing Anton now because Tom is clearly a lost cause.

"A black mass," he says.

"Not necessarily," Tom cuts in again, seeing an opportunity to show off his own expertise despite it going against his intended strategy of allowing me to implicate myself, "A black mass would only be carried out at midnight, but the sacrifice of the hen and rooster is used in other rituals as well. There's something else going on here and she knows what it is."

Anton doesn't really have a chance to consider this because that's when there's a scream from downstairs.

CHAPTER 8

A Perfect Circle

I run to the door, expecting Tom and Anton to do the same, but Tom grabs my arm and pulls me back.

"It's too late," he says.

I look at Anton. Surely he will step in. This is a perfect hero moment for him, to the point I even wonder whether he set it up. Tom is the crazy one here who barged into my house uninvited, and now Anton can come to my rescue. I don't want him to necessarily; I pull myself out of Tom's grip easily enough. I'm just surprised by Anton's in-activity. He looks different and I see something on his face that I realise I never saw on his TV show. He looks incredibly scared.

"Trust me," says Tom, "Do not go down there."

I do trust him. I don't know why, but I know that if Anton had told me not to respond to the scream from downstairs, I would be halfway to the kitchen by now. I believe in Tom enough to at least hear him out, although I suspect there will be the usual monologues and mansplaining to wade through before I get to the truth.

The scream sounded male. So either Steve or Lee. I feel bad for saying so, but I hope it was Lee because then at least Steve and Beth are down there to rescue him from whatever it is. That's not really why I hope it was Lee. I mostly just want Steve to be okay because he's the only one who was nice to me, but that doesn't make me a bad person, does it? I can't hear anything now. What could have happened? There was all kinds of heavy equipment down there, so maybe Beth just dropped a tripod on Lee's foot or something. But if it was something like that, why did Tom say we can't leave?

Tom swings his rucksack off his back and drops it, clattering to the floor. I can hear a woman screaming now. Maybe Beth or Chloe. I catch myself hoping it's Chloe, which is unfair, really. I also catch myself really not wanting to go downstairs. There are other sounds now too. There are bangs and crashes like furniture being pushed over or someone being pushed into furniture. Then there's this other sound I can't really describe, like some kind of animal is down there with them.

Tom empties the contents of his bag over the

floor. So much junk I can't even begin to describe it all. The floorboards at his feet look like one of those memory games where there's a bunch of random items and then one of them is taken away and you have to remember what was there, but Tom's version would be impossible. There are heavy-duty builder's tools mixed in with pens, pencils and paper and then a few old-looking books. Mixed in with those are some more esoteric items like amulets and crystals and even an ornate dagger. Then there are random household items like bleach, cotton wool balls and a few other things you might find under a sink or in a bathroom. Tom scatters his inventory all over the floor, then picks out a large hammer and some nails.

"What are you doing?" I ask, because someone has to.

"Protecting us," says Tom as he surveys the room, looking for something.

"I'm going to check on the others," Anton declares with a concern for his crew I wasn't sure he was capable of.

"Don't go down those stairs!"

Tom raises the hammer as he says this and whether or not he means to, he's coming across as more than a little threatening right now.

"Five seconds ago you wanted me to leave!" Anton argues.

Tom seems to disregard this and goes back to looking for whatever he was looking for, muttering, "You don't want to see whatever's down there."

"I'm coming with you," I announce, because whatever made those people scream like that I'm not convinced we're any safer up here with this hammer-wielding psycho.

It's funny how quickly my trust in Tom disappears once he's armed.

Tom doesn't say anything this time. He's found a spot on the floor he likes the look of, and now he's on his knees lining up a nail in what looks to be the dead centre of the room.

I join Anton and move to the door, expecting him to follow. To be honest, I'm expecting him to go first, but he's frozen in place. He's watching Tom.

There's another sound from downstairs now. Someone is crying. Sobbing, in fact. I listen closely, trying to work out who it could be from the sound of their sobs.

I'm startled by a BANG as Tom hammers the nail into the floorboard. He hits it a few more times but doesn't drive it all the way through into the wood. Then he takes a large roll of twine from his pocket and ties one end around the tip of the nail. Strangely, it's this relatively sedate action that snaps Anton out of his trance and he walks over to the door.

"Are you alright down there?" Anton shouts through the doorway.

There is no response from downstairs. Anton is edging through the doorway, moving closer to the stairs but not quite leaving the room.

I'm fascinated by Tom's actions now. He's stretched out the twine to a length of about two metres and then cut it off with a penknife. Now he's tying a piece of chalk to the end. He pulls the twine taut and gets down onto his knees. Using the nail as an anchor, he draws on the floorboards in chalk with the twine stretched to its full extent. As he slowly makes his way around the room on his hands and knees, he leaves a white trail behind him and the end result is a perfect chalk circle.

Anton has hesitated in the doorway, listening. The sobbing has stopped.

"Steve!" he shouts, then, "Chloe!"

I wonder if the order he shouted the names bears any significance, like perhaps they are the two he most relies on to come to his rescue in situations like this. I would imagine Chloe would be first to run in any kind of emergency, but maybe I've underestimated her.

Tom shortens the length of twine, then reattaches the chalk and draws a second circle around ten centimetres inside the first. I could watch this all day, but then I see my dad watching too, except he's watching me.

"Let's just go down there," I suggest to Anton, mostly because I can't bear to have Dad stare at me like that any longer because I know what he must be thinking.

Anton looks at me and for the first time since I met him I feel like I'm looking at the real human person behind all the bullshit. He looks lost and frightened and a little sad. I almost want to hug him, which is very out of character for me, as you well know.

"What if he's right?" Anton says.

"Right about what?" I ask. "You heard the same things I did. It sounded like they were in trouble. They're your crew, you need to check on them!"

Anton looks at Tom again. He's now detached the chalk from the twine and is drawing a pentagram inside the inner circle. He draws free-form now and yet the lines of the pentagram are so perfectly straight they look as though they could have been printed onto the floor by a computer. The concentration on Tom's face along with his furrowed, sweating brow implies this feat is not accomplished without considerable effort on his part.

Anton turns back to me and says, "If he's right, we can't go down there. If he's wrong, we'll know soon enough."

He steps away from the doorway and joins Tom in the circle.

"I'm going downstairs!" I say, but neither of them are listening.

Anton looks down at Tom's drawing and asks, "A protection circle?"

Tom breaks his chalk in two and hands Anton half.

"Do you remember the inscription?" he asks.

Anton nods, taking the chalk. There's the sound

of chalk hitting wood like drumming but the rhythm is erratic. The two men scrawl something in the space between the inner and outer circles. They work in opposite directions and the ease of this process is unmistakable. There's no discussion, no consultation and after watching them for a moment I know exactly why. They've done this together before and likely many times.

I feel like it's my birthday party and I'm sitting alone in a corner while everyone else talks to each other. I feel like I did almost every day of school. I feel alienated; like I don't belong here. It's a familiar feeling in this house. I look at the stairs. I could just leave them to it. I don't need to be here. As long as they fix the problem. I don't even need to do anything with the house, particularly, I just need to stop seeing Dad everywhere. But that's buying into my own fiction. I need to remember why we're really here.

"I'm still here!" I shout, trying to sound like an annoyed client but probably coming off more like the spoilt birthday girl, not getting enough attention. "Remember me?"

Tom finishes his half of the circle and stands. He doesn't look at me. Anton is still scrawling on the floorboards, slower than Tom. He's clearly thinking about it, unsure exactly what he's doing. Occasionally he looks over at Tom's side of the circle, presumably to check he's done it properly. I look at their work. There are strange symbols that appear almost mathematical, with their straight lines joining into smaller circles. Between them are words I don't recognise. Some of the text is illegible and I wonder if it's just bad handwriting by Tom and Anton or whether the words also include unfamiliar characters. I can make out only one coherent word in the entire circle and that reads "ASTAROTH".

Tom reaches into his bag again and though I find it hard to believe there is anything else in there, he extracts a handful of large candles. He places the candles on the points of the pentagram. It's a slow process because he has to use a lighter to melt the base of the candle first and can only stand the candle up on the point when enough wax has dripped onto the floor to hold it.

Neither Anton nor Tom has acknowledged me since I spoke. I decide to at least make a show of leaving and I move towards the door.

"Coralie, stay here," says Anton, shaking his head.

"You can't expect me to stay up here if you're not going to tell me what's going on!" I say as I step out of the doorway and over to top of the stairs.

"Coralie!" Anton shouts.

"Let her go," says Tom, which I immediately resent.

I look back into the room. Tom is on the third candle now. Anton has finished his half of the text in the outer circle and is looking up at me. At least he's acknowledging that I'm here now.

I'm at the top of the stairs. There's no light on

the landing and no windows, so the stairs themselves are dark. There is light at the bottom of the stairs, but I can only see the bare hallway floorboards and no sign of what has been happening down there. That shadow doesn't seem familiar though. It's a black shape, like a long coat has been hung from the top of the wall at the bottom of the stairs. That's what it must be, someone's coat. There are probably picture hooks there from when there were photo frames hung on the wall and someone decided to hang their coat from one, most likely Steve, it's such a Steve thing to do. That's what it is, it's just Steve's coat. It's the classic mistake of thinking you've seen a figure in your room at night but then you turn the light on and it's just some piled up clothes that look like a person in the dark. Then the clothes move.

It's not a coat because it's moving. Whoever it is must have their back pressed against the wall as they sidle up the stairs. I try to tell myself the coat is being blown in the wind or perhaps the light has changed, but then I hear the footsteps.

Tom's head snaps to attention the moment the sound hits his ears. Anton reacts a split-second later and almost leaps over to the door.

He yells at me, "Into the circle! Quickly!"

I look at the door again and tell him, "There's someone on the stairs."

"Light the candles!" shouts Tom, throwing a lighter to Anton.

Anton catches the lighter and with frantic

desperation he turns back to the circle then tries and fails to light the first candle. Meanwhile, Tom has placed five silver cups around the circumference of the circle in the spaces between the points of the pentagram. He takes a flask from the bits and pieces on the floor, unscrews the cap and pours a measure of what looks like water into each of the cups. Anton is having better luck with the lighter now and is onto the next candle. All this time the footsteps are slowly advancing, louder and closer with each step.

I can't see the shape anymore. I've backed away towards the door. I want to look and reassure them, but I don't. I want to peer down the stairs again and tell them it's just Steve, but I'm not going to. I know it's not Steve. There's something off about the sound of the footsteps. I don't know whether it's the slow pace of the steps or the unnatural thud they produce, but it doesn't sound like a person. Maybe they're injured, I wonder, but surely they would have called out by now? No, it's not a person. The shape isn't moving like a person either.

"Coralie, come on!" shouts Anton.

I turn back and see he's lit all the candles but one. He's hovering over it with the lighter, but he hesitates, waiting for me. That last footstep was louder than the others. I think there are three, maybe four steps left before they're on the landing.

"Is this still part of your show?" I ask, and I try to make it sound like an accusation, but I don't really believe it.

THUD

Tom has filled the cups and is standing in the centre of the circle.

THUD

"Light the candle," he instructs Anton.

THUD

"If I light this candle and you're not in the circle, I'm not sure it will protect you," Anton warns me.

THUD

"It won't," Tom clarifies, "Light the candle."

The footsteps are on the landing now. I'm in the doorway. I hesitate because I think whatever was on the stairs will be the truth Tom and Anton won't tell me and this way I will find out for my-self. I hesitate because ever since Tom turned up I've been thinking maybe this is a con and he and Anton planned it this way from the start so if I do what they say I'm handing control over to them. I hesitate because I'm not supposed to believe in the thing I saw on the stairs. The footsteps are faster now, two at a time.

THUD-THUD

"I don't understand what's happening," I say, because I really don't.

I look to my dad for reassurance, but he's just staring at me, smiling his strange smile again.

THUD-THUD

"Do it!" shouts Tom.

THUD-THUD

Anton flicks the lighter on and there's a spark

but no accompanying flame.

THUD-THUD

Anton tries the lighter again. This time it works.

THUD-THUD

I'm in the room, but I turn back to the door again. The landing is dark, almost pitch black, but I can see movement.

THUD-THUD

I see it more clearly now. It's not a person. The shadow is a mass of shifting, undulating shapes. I don't understand what I'm looking at. Just a couple more steps and it will be in the light.

THUD-THUD

I dash across the room and into the circle.

Anton lights the candle.

The footsteps cease.

No one walks through the door.

The room is silent and there's something different about it. After a moment I realise what it is. Dad isn't in the room anymore.

CHAPTER 9

The Plan

"Where is it?" whispers Anton after a full minute of silence has passed.

"Quiet!" whispers Tom, although his whisper is so loud he may as well be shouting.

Anton looks at Tom, so I do too. I don't know exactly when the power shifted in this relationship but there's definitely been a switch. Since he began drawing the circle Tom has taken charge. I don't like being told what to do, but I appreciate Tom's sincerity. It does at least feel like he's trying to solve the problem, even if he has his own reasons for wanting to solve it. That last part is the issue. Should I choose to believe I was in danger outside the circle, and given what I saw I have to give this possibility some serious consideration, then I also have to believe that Tom had no interest in making sure I was safe. I'm also concerned that he's made Dad go away, which is ridiculous because that's obviously what I wanted, but the irony about having him leave at the expense of me being trapped in his room again is not lost on me.

"Okay," he says eventually, "I think it's gone."

We stand in silence for a moment longer, none of us quite ready to believe it. I saw something in the dark, but I'm not going to tell them. I'll tell you because I know you, but not them. They wouldn't believe me, anyway.

"Guys!" Anton shouts, "Steve! Chloe! What the fuck are you playing at?"

I think Anton must be in denial, but when he moves to the edge of the circle, I wonder if maybe he really thinks his crew is down there waiting for us. It would be a bold move for the crew of a ghost hunting TV show to arrange a prank like this. If it was a prank, then they must realise their jobs are at stake. I can't see Lee and Chloe being up for it, and even Steve seemed loyal to Anton. Beth is the most likely suspect as she doesn't seem to like him much, but I'm basing that on her not seeming to like anyone. Either way, the prank theory seems unlikely, but I don't voice this opinion because Anton looks like it might crush him.

Tom steps forward and holds out his arm in front of Anton. He shakes his head.

"I have to know if they're okay," Anton pleads.

"You know you can't leave this circle. Not until we're sure."

Anton's reaction is a little out of character. This morning he dismissed Tom as an amateur, then moments before I entered the circle he was fully on board with Team Tom and seemed entirely committed to the idea that staying in this room is more important than checking on his team. I wonder if his earlier bravado was for my benefit and intended to ensure Tom didn't dominant the proceedings. Perhaps now the reality of the situation is setting in and he's wondering what really has happened downstairs. Or maybe he genuinely believed it was one of his colleagues thumping up the stairs and was hoping for an opportunity to further undermine his competitor. Either way, despite Tom's confidence, I feel more closely aligned with Anton, as he is at least closer to my level of uncertainty and confusion. What's strange is the earlier animosity between the two men seems to be as absent as my dead dad.

"Anton, I need you to tell me what's happening," I say, and then I decide a gentler approach is required and I add, "If this is a set-up I won't be mad, I just need you to tell me."

Anton looks at me and the over-confident, arrogant eyes are back when he replies, "You think I'm responsible for this?"

"Wouldn't be the first time," says Tom and I don't think he's joking.

I was wrong about the animosity not being

there.

"Is that true?" I ask, aware this may not be the right time, but also it's the perfect time. "Have you faked stuff before?"

"I've never faked anything," says Anton.

"Exaggerated, maybe?" is Tom's less than helpful suggestion.

Sensing a crisis, Anton ignores Tom and looks at me. "You have to understand it is very difficult to fund research into paranormal activity. This is why your friend Tom still has a day job. That's why I've taken the science-as-entertainment route, because it's the only way to fund extensive research into cases like yours."

"That's how you justify it, is it?" Tom won't let this go, "So you fake a ghost every week but it's okay because your wages are going into 'legitimate' research."

Anton turns to face Tom now and responds, "The show is the legitimate research."

"So you're saying you have to make your research entertaining," concludes Tom, "Which is a long way of saying you fake everything."

"Stop!" I shout, because I don't know what else to do to get them to notice me again. "Just be straight with me. That's your crew downstairs. Are you saying they weren't in on this? Something really has happened to them?"

Anton turns back to me and says, "If they are in on this, and I'm not saying we rule that out, I wasn't part of it."

"But you won't check? I don't get it. This morning you said he was trolling you."

"Trolling?" Tom scoffs.

"Here's the thing," says Anton, suggesting he's making his conclusions as he's saying them aloud to me. "He told you he didn't believe your problem existed. When the guy who doesn't believe in ghosts tells you there's something to worry about, that's a fucking good reason to start worrying. I've only seen Tom this scared once before—"

"Don't tell her anything," says Tom. "You can't give away information like that. They can use it. We need to understand what's going on here first."

By 'they' I'm not sure whether he means me or whatever entity we're now dealing with in this house.

"We're going to have to trust her," Anton says to Tom. "She's in the circle with us. If there was something wrong, she wouldn't have been able to get in. Would she?"

Tom considers this. He looks at me and he looks at the circle, inspecting the circumference and the markings to make sure everything is in order. He even looks at my feet, presumably to ensure I'm standing on the floorboards inside the circle and not somehow levitating above it. I'm not entirely sure what I'm being accused of here, but I don't like it.

"You let her in before the circle closed," says Tom.

"So we'll never know," Anton replies, clearly losing his patience, "This has always been your problem, Tom, you pull this shit out of your toolbox like it has meaning but you don't have a fucking clue what you're doing."

"I know enough to understand these are not what I would call ideal research conditions."

"They never are."

"Certainly not with you around."

And then I remember something I meant to say earlier, before the footsteps on the stairs.

"I didn't realise you two knew each other," I say.

"He's my brother," says Anton as if it's obvious.

Before I can really take this in, Tom says, "Shh!"

We do as he says, and then I hear it. There's a creaking sound. I've heard it in this room before, but after everything that's happened, I decide not to point this out again. We listen and the creaking continues, fading out but then resuming almost immediately. After a while it stops sounding like a creaking and sounds like something else; something human. The creaking from above could well be a groan.

"We should try to communicate," says Anton with confidence.

Anton is used to spirits making sounds, and he's back on familiar ground. I wait for the 'one for yes and two for no' instruction.

"I'm not sure there's anything to communicate with," Tom replies, still staring at the ceiling.

"You can't seriously put on your skeptic hat after what you just made us do," Anton argues, and it's a fair point.

"I don't think there are ghosts here. This is something else. Demons, black magic maybe, but not ghosts."

"So you don't believe in ghosts but you believe in black magic?" I say with the most contentious voice I can manage, which isn't very contentious given the circumstances.

"I believe in occult science," Tom explains, "There are forces in the universe that we don't understand. We access those forces through a science sometimes referred to as black magic, but the research is old and out of date. I'm not sure any of it means what we think it means."

"Get ready for the omelette-in-a-tumble-dryer speech," says Anton, ignoring Tom to focus on the ceiling.

"The what?" I ask, genuinely believing I misheard.

"There are records of occult practitioners producing results using rituals from ancients texts," Tom begins, "I just don't believe those results were intentional. These rituals have been passed down through generations, but there was never sufficient scientific research into the cause and effect. It was all based on faith, the same as any other religion and because it produced results the validity or the intention of those rituals was never questioned. John Dee, Aleister Crowley, Kenneth Anger, they all practiced this stuff and most of it was nonsense but some of it worked. That means there was something there, it just wasn't the something that early occultists thought it was. If you put all the ingredients for an omelette into a tumble dryer, you will produce a result, but it won't look much like an omelette."

"That is a strange analogy," I say, because it is and also kind of distracts from the point rather than reinforcing it because now all I can think about is what the inside of that tumble dryer would look like.

"Someone wants something to happen here," Tom persists. "They killed two birds outside this house, which means they're serious. Whatever they've invoked has either caused harm to Anton's crew or it wants us to think it has. I'm assuming we all heard the same thing - a male scream, then a female scream, then crashing and banging and finally the sobbing? That's what you heard, isn't it?"

I nod in agreement, then add, "And the footsteps."

"Yes, and then the footsteps on the stairs," Tom agrees and I feel like I just got teacher's approval, "Anton, you heard the same, didn't you?"

Anton nods, then asks "Could it be anything else?"

"You tell me," says Tom, "They're your crew. Would they set up something like this?"

We've been over this before but then it is the only rational explanation, so I join Tom in looking at Anton with expectation in my folded arms.

"They've pranked me before, if that's what you're implying," he says, defensive.

That's interesting, I'd love to hear those stories. I hope I can ask Steve about it later. I'm so delighted by this idea I rush to decide that this is what has happened, but Anton is still talking.

"I've been working with the same crew for a couple of years now. They were handpicked after some unpleasant experiences with individuals the production companies have landed me with in the past. I needed people I could trust, and I trust them. Even if one or two of them are capable of putting on a performance, I doubt they'd go as far as killing a chicken. Most of them are vegan."

"The birds," says Tom, thinking, "That's almost the part that worries me the most."

I find it hard to believe that two dead chickens are more worrying than potentially four dead or injured humans and a malevolent entity on the stairs, but I don't have time to really consider it because Tom is looking at me now.

"Are you certain your father didn't own these animals?"

"I don't know," I say honestly. "I told you, Dad and I weren't close. I hadn't been here for years. It doesn't seem like him but to be honest, I barely knew him."

Anton frowns at this, and I suddenly remember I've given both men different stories. I'll have to be careful what I say going forward. Then again, does it matter anymore? I can't even see Dad anymore.

"There could still be an explanation," Anton argues. "They didn't have to have been killed in the garden. What if they were chased from another garden? What if they were killed as random acts of violence and the heads thrown over the fence? I know it seems meaningful because of our reasons for being here but it could still be a coincidence."

Anton is doing Tom's job here, and he's actually pretty convincing.

"Everything could always be a coincidence," says Tom and I prepare myself for another omelette analogy.

"Or," says Anton, pausing for effect, "There is the possibility that you killed the birds and brought the heads to convince us to allow you to take part."

A scowl crosses Tom's face, but he reins it in before he says, "Park the birds for a moment. Let's go back to the sounds we all heard. There are dozens of likely explanations. They could be testing their equipment. Maybe they played back an old episode at full volume? Maybe the sounds are unconnected? Someone gets a splinter from one of the rotting door frames and yells out. Someone else just happens to have had some bad news and is sitting on the stairs sobbing. Yet another person is walking up the stairs, but then they hear us talking and assume we're filming so they sneak back down again. Coincidence stacked on top of coincidence. Unlikely, but possible. What's your take, Anton?"

Tom looks at Anton. Anton glances up at the

ceiling again, but the groaning-or-creaking has stopped. He takes a few paces around the edge of the circle, in full TV ghost hunter mode again.

"I don't think we can rule out demonic intervention. There is a certain heaviness in the atmosphere," he says, "I can sense a presence in this house and it doesn't want us here."

Tom shakes his head. "I didn't ask for your opening monologue, I want your scientific opinion."

Anton hesitates for a moment, then he says, "My scientific opinion is that the only person who could possibly be responsible for this is you."

That would be why he hesitated. I'm watching two children playing a game but one of them wants to bend the rules and the other won't let him. Tom looks incredulous. I'm suddenly more invested in this exchange than I am in cleansing the house of spirits.

Anton continues, "You're the only one who saw anything outside. You brought the severed chicken heads from elsewhere, it's the most likely explanation. You had time to chat to my crew before you came up here and though I'd like to think they'd be above a bribe, I know a couple would do it to get at me."

Tom looks at me now and says, "This is why I work alone. The moment paranormal evidence presents itself everyone wants to blame each other for setting it up."

"You asked for my scientific opinion," argues

Anton, "And you were the one who was so quick to blame my crew."

"We have to consider all factors," says Tom. "The problems in this house did not begin on my arrival. Coralie, where's your dad right now?"

I look around just in case, then I answer honestly, "I can't see him."

Tom nods as if expecting this response, "It's because of the circle."

"So the circle stops us from seeing ghosts?" says Anton. "How convenient."

I glare at Anton, remembering where we were when Tom came in. He never believed I could see Dad in the first place.

"Let's assume the worst-case scenario for a moment," says Tom, ignoring Anton and looking at me again, but now in a way that worries me.

"That she's pranking both of us?" Anton suggests. "I can certainly see that."

"No, that this is really happening," Tom states. "Coralie really sees her dead father walking around in front of her. Some kind of occult rite has been executed this morning outside, possibly even inside, this house. Your crew is hurt, probably dead and whatever did that to them is in the building and the only thing protecting us is this circle, which we now cannot leave."

Tom allows us to take all of this in. When he says it like that and then I remember the sounds from downstairs and the shape in the doorway, it's all very convincing. There is something wrong with this house and it's far worse than the ghost of my dad. Anton has a defiant look on his face, like he's still not quite prepared to believe it. I'd never realised how complicated belief can be. It's as if Anton feels he's conceding something to his brother by declaring his belief in something he has built his career on believing in. I knew Anton exaggerated and maybe faked a few experiences, but I had always assumed he truly believed in the basic principles of paranormal investigation, but maybe not. Meanwhile, Tom appears to have weaponised the very idea of belief to use against his brother, and I wonder if that's the only reason he's here.

"So," Tom says eventually, "What are we going to do about it?"

CHAPTER 10

Scars

"We wait," Anton suggests. "My demonologist, Carter, is on his way. He usually arrives late so I'm guessing he'll be here in the next half an hour."

"Oh, a demonologist!" scoffs Tom. "He'll save us with his extensive knowledge of made-up bull-shit!"

"I just mean there will be someone else coming in," Anton explains, glaring at Tom. "Another person. If he walks through that door like nothing's happened we'll know there's no danger and we can leave the circle."

"Okay," Tom admits, "That actually makes sense."

I can't quite believe what I'm hearing. The more

time passes without incident, the more I begin to question what we heard happening downstairs and the more I begin to question whether anything happened the more ridiculous it seems to stand in the middle of a hastily scrawled chalk circle. However, that I can no longer see my dad in the room suggests there is some power here, so maybe I should just keep my mouth shut and let the experts take charge. Tom appears to have the most pragmatic approach so maybe I should just let him do his thing? Anton is behaving differently now too, less like his on-screen persona and more like a ghost hunting professional, like his brother.

His brother. It still seems strange to think of the two men as brothers. I think about the story Anton told in his book about being locked in the abandoned house by his brother. That was Tom. Tom has his own version of that story. The connection is obvious now but I was so focused on their differences I never saw them as coming the same place. I want to ask about it but now is not the time.

"We can't just stand here waiting," I say, more to myself but I've said it to the room now so I have to follow through, "There must be something we can be doing."

"She wants us to leave the circle," says Tom.

I sense Tom has turned on me. Gone is the polite awkwardness with which he first spoke to me that night in the pub. His eyes are full of distrust when he looks at me now; he looks at me the way Anton was looking at me earlier. I suspect it's because I saw him crying earlier. I saw him vulnerable and hurt because of something I did, so now he's trying to get back at me somehow. His distrust is emotional and mean-spirited rather than based on anything I've actually done. At least that's what I tell myself. I can see this version of Tom locking his brother in an abandoned house. Let's say he has genuine suspicions. I don't know what he suspects me of doing beyond killing two chickens, and I don't know what he thinks the implications are if I did. I just know that if there is danger in this house, then Tom seems like my best hope of survival and I need to get him back onside.

"Tom, leave her alone," says Anton, suddenly my knight in shining armour.

I suppose I should consider myself lucky that Anton is on my team right now. If he was looking at me, the way Tom is, I'd be worried they would burn me at the stake. That's one way this could end, with me tied to a gatepost in the garden while Tom and Anton set fire to the junk at my feet. After some of the things that have happened today, this doesn't seem too far-fetched at all.

"There are things we can do, Coralie," says Tom, "I'll be honest. I think you know more about this than you're letting on. I don't say this to be cruel or because I'm afraid but because I want to help. If you want me to help, you need to help me first. You need to tell me about your dad."

I don't believe a word of that last part. I think he is being cruel because he sees an opportunity to hurt me.

"I'd like to know whether your dad ever practiced black magic in this house," Tom continues, "Anything that you remember."

"She would've told us," argues Anton, still playing the part of my defence lawyer in our little impromptu trial.

"Not necessarily," says Tom. "It wasn't known that George Lutz was an occultist until his son Daniel talked about it over 30 years later."

I know Tom wants me to ask who George Lutz is and I'm about to do it just to speed things up, but then Anton does it for me.

"George who?"

"Amityville!" Tom shouts at Anton, "How is that you can call this your job?"

I see now why neither of them told me they were related. There's so much bitterness and bad blood here. Tom, the serious practitioner who approaches ghost investigations like academic science experiments but lacks the funding to pursue fully the results he requires. Meanwhile, his brother makes a mockery of his science by making it an entertainment and is awarded a successful career and a degree of prestige Tom can only dream of. Tom is delighted to call Anton out on his lack of knowledge, especially in front of me.

"He used to draw circles on the floor," I say because as much as I want Tom on my side I don't think I can bear a condescending retelling of the Amityville ghost story at his brother's expense.

"Circles like this?" asks Tom, indicating the chalk circle he we are still standing in.

"The same place, but they looked different," I explain. "He'd sit me or my mum in the middle, sometimes both of us. And then he'd start."

Anton looks hurt, maybe a little betrayed, after he stood up for me. He already knows I'd been more honest with Tom than I had with him and I think he realises I told him what he needed to hear. He should really reflect on that because there's a reason I convinced Tom to come here with what was mostly the truth and Anton with lies. He's not the reflecting type, and I'm losing him again. Meanwhile, Tom is talking to me like a concerned parent rather than Witchfinder General, so that's progress. I consider the possibility that there may not be a way to balance the two men. One of them will always distrust me, but as long as the other believes, then we can move forward.

"Start what?" asks Tom. "I know this may be difficult but you have to tell me everything, it's important."

"Everything bad that happened to me happened in a pentagram inside a chalk circle. That's why I hesitated before I stepped into yours."

I'm not sure if it is really why I hesitated, but it was such a convenient idea that as soon as I thought about it I had to throw it out there. Aren't you proud of me? I'm certainly proud of myself. Suggesting that the circle is somehow triggering is perfect because it explains everything. Every lie

I've told and every action they don't understand now makes sense because I suffered so much pain in this room and they're making me relive it. They both look sad for me now. They have achieved balance after all.

"Did he do this alone?" Tom asks, speaking slowly and in a low voice because he knows this could be a triggering question and he's asking anyway.

"Sometimes. He had friends. They would come over to the house and drink and tell jokes. When I was younger, I used to sit in bed listening to them, thinking Dad was having a party. After the first time, I understood that when his friends were here eventually they would come upstairs and eventually the laughing would stop."

I'm going too far. Were there others? I don't really remember. The parties were from before, weren't they? When Dad was happy. I think I've conflated two memories, but it's too late now.

"Do you know if any of these people your father brought in to…" he's not sure how to finish the sentence so he lets it hang there, "Are any of them still alive?"

"I have no idea," I say, trying and failing to picture the faces of the men I've invented, "I suppose some of them were younger than him."

"So that's it," exclaims Anton, "That explains the chickens. Maybe it was his dying wish that they carry out this ritual. Or maybe he's not the ringleader here, there could be someone else who is determined to finish what they started."

"I'm sorry to ask this, Coralie," Tom continues. "I need to know what he was doing to you. What did he think he was going to achieve?"

I think before I respond, although part of my hesitation is that I want them to think this is hard for me. The other part is that it is genuinely hard. I haven't really talked about what Dad did. I've lied to both of them, more to one than the other, but there have been so many lies and now I've lost track of what I said to who. I suppose it's time to tell the truth, or at least something closer to the truth. At least Dad isn't here watching me right now and if he is, not being able to see him makes it easy to pretend. I don't think I could do this with him watching.

"Dad thought there was something inside me. Something evil."

"Was there?" asks Tom without hesitation.

I feel like Tom was expecting this. He's been on Dad's side all along. I wonder if he started piecing it together when we met at the pub. Could I have underestimated him that much? The sacrifices in the garden seemed to have cemented whatever theory he formed then and now he's made his mind up. No, I can see from the way he looks at me he hasn't decided yet. I think he's a little afraid of me, but only because I hurt him once. I think he's holding onto the hope of saving me too. He reminds me of Dad in some ways. I think they would have been friends.

"This is exactly why I didn't tell you any of this before," I say, voicing my concerns. "I know what you're thinking. You're just like him."

"I'm not jumping to any conclusions," Tom argues in his defence, "I just need the truth."

The truth. Should I give them a bit more? I have to be careful with it. It's like chemistry, too much and it will poison them, not enough and they will give up on me, but if I give them just the right amount of truth, maybe they'll help me finish this.

"It was because of my mum," I explain. "She was a witch."

I wait for their shocked reactions, but of course they barely react at all.

"You mean she practiced Wicca," Tom corrects me, which is the other reaction I expected.

I nod. "That's how they met, in an occult book shop. There was some kind of group that used to meet in the shop after hours and they were both members. They performed rituals together. I get the impression Mum was more into it than Dad. I think Dad got into it to meet women and once it had worked, he lost interest. For Mum, it was her whole life. She thought magic governed everything. If she stubbed her toe or something, she would blame the ritual she'd done the night before and pick out some part of it she knew she'd done wrong. It wasn't just her either, she would see someone trip in the street and she'd take out her charms and would sit cross-legged on the pavement as she chanted to whatever force she thought had made it happen. I think if you get deep into that stuff and you change your life to fit around it then it can make the world a tough place to live in."

"How did your father react to all this?" asks Tom.

"He was understanding at first. He would lose his patience sometimes, like I remember we were going to the theatre on Christmas to see the panto and we were late because Mum had a bad feeling when she left the house. In the end we were so late they wouldn't let us in and we missed the show, which I was secretly happy about, but it really pissed Dad off. He wouldn't take it out on her, though. He would shout and swear and make everyone aware he was pissed off, but it was never directed at her. I think he believed the same way she did but when I came along he realised, it wasn't practical for them to both live their lives that way."

"What went wrong?" Anton asks, obviously keen to skip to the trauma.

"Something happened to Mum," I explain. "She changed."

"How?" asks Tom. "You must be precise. Was it a physical change? A mental change?"

"It became physical, but that's not how it started. At first I just noticed she was mean. She was a really kind person; people used to talk about how kind she was all the time. For most of my childhood she never raised her voice to me, even when she probably should've done. Then one day she just snapped at me for no reason. It happened more and more often, until I hated being around her because she acted like she didn't want me there. It suddenly felt like I couldn't do anything right because whatever we were doing, she'd find a reason to scream at me. Some of the things she used to say... they weren't things a child should ever have to hear. Sometimes she hit me. That was when Dad intervened. It reached the point where it felt like he wouldn't leave her alone with me. He couldn't be there all the time, though. He couldn't be there in the night."

I pause here, taking a measure of how much more truth I can add, then I tell the worst part, "One night I woke up, and she was standing over my bed holding a kitchen knife. She saw me looking at her and she just dropped the knife and walked away. I know how this sounds but I wish I'd never told Dad about the knife."

"It sounds like a case of demonic possession," Anton pronounces with a smugness that betrays his pride at having been first to reach this conclusion.

I like how he calls it 'a case of demonic possession' as if that somehow distances him from the reality of what happened. I suppose as a ghost hunter he's not used to dealing with a victim who is still alive and standing in front of him.

"It could be depression," suggests Tom, instantly deflating Anton's ego, "Schizophrenia, bipolar disorder - any number of things."

"We'll never have the exact diagnosis," Anton

continues, unwilling to allow Tom to steal this minor victory from him. "Regardless of her mental state, your dad must have believed his wife was possessed. That's what happened, isn't it?"

I nod, deciding to let Anton fill in a few of the gaps for me.

"I think I'm beginning to understand," he says like a TV detective about to deliver his concluding remarks, "Your dad notices your mum acting weird and he assumes the worst. Not knowing where else to turn, he takes matters into his own hands. Unfortunately, exorcisms can be violent and destructive if you've not had the proper training."

I say nothing and allow him a minute to believe he knows my entire story now.

"What did you think, Coralie?" Anton continues, "What did you think happened to her?"

Time for another truth bomb.

"If you knew what he'd done to me, you wouldn't be asking that question."

"He's not asking about the methods," says Tom, suddenly backing up his brother, "Do you believe your dad was onto something?"

"I was a child," I say, and I try to cry here but it doesn't really work, I need to build up to it, "I didn't know what was going on with her, not really. Like you said, it could have been caused by any number of things."

"So you truly don't believe there was anything evil inside her?" Tom continues.

"I don't think she deserved what Dad did to her." I say knowing full well I'm avoiding the question but I haven't decided how I'm going to answer.

"What about you?" asks Anton, redirecting the conversation to my experiences, which is ultimately where I want it to be, even if I'm not looking forward to this bit.

"I don't think I deserved it either," I say, dragging the interrogation out a little longer.

"But you knew there was nothing inside you," Anton continues. "You knew you weren't possessed by demonic forces so it follows that your mother wasn't either."

I see what he's done there. Anton has reached what he assumes must have been my conclusion by way of his own. I look at Tom for his reaction. He seems lost in thought, staring at the floorboards as if he remembers dropping the answers he's looking for, but now he can't see them.

"We're not getting anywhere with this," Anton he says to Tom, suddenly frustrated.

"There is a school of thought that suggests the bond between family members can be a powerful catalyst for paranormal events," Tom says to Anton as if I'm no longer in the room. "That could explain why hauntings often appear to centre around trauma. Here we have violence caused by a father to his own daughter. Blood spilled by blood in this very room. Who knows what anomalies that could cause?"

Strangely, it's Anton who now looks unconvinced.

"Have you experienced anything unusual since leaving this house?" Tom asks, skipping ahead, "Before you saw your dad's ghost, I mean."

"There was…" no, if I tell him he'll want to see, "No, nothing."

Tom leaps on the hesitation like a cat pouncing on prey. "What were you going to say just then?"

I look to Anton for support but he knows Tom is onto something and he wants to find out what it is. I suppose I'll have to show them eventually so it may as well be now.

"There was something wrong with my body," I tell them, hoping it's enough. "A girl I was with noticed it. I had so many hang-ups about the way I looked back then, I'd never really thought of it. We were in bed. I suppose it must have been the first time. She was horrified."

"Show me," says Tom, as if it's the easiest thing in the world for me to do.

"Hold on," Anton interrupts, although I think he's just making a show of being my knight again because I think he really wants to see as much as Tom does, "You don't have to do anything you don't want to do."

"She does if we're going to get out of this," Tom insists. "I need to see it."

"I contained it," I explain as I unbutton my shirt, "Better than my dad ever could."

I take off my shirt, and I show them my back. I turn slowly, so they can see the tattoos and how they spiral around my abdomen in a mosaic of symbols and arcane words; words like "AS-TAROTH". This is my first lie revealed. I know more about what's happening than I've told them, but neither of them would have come if I'd been honest. They needed to believe they were saving me from something I didn't understand, and they did.

I continue to turn and now they see it. The tattoos converge around a saucer-sized area of flesh on my back. It's hard for me to see in a mirror so I don't know exactly what it looks like, but I'm told there are three scars there.

I think back to that night when I first found out about the scars. She'd been so kind to me and I felt comfortable around her. It had been difficult to have her see my body when no one had before, but she let me do it in my own time. The first couple of times we just lay in bed together, me fully clothed. The third time I showed her. She was concerned when she saw the scars, but not repulsed. She said they were almost beautiful and when I asked her to describe them she said they were like two eyes and a mouth, like a face. She asked what had happened. I told her I didn't know, because I didn't even know they were there. I was trying to remember, thinking I'd perhaps repressed a memory of one of the many injuries Dad had given me. But then she screamed. She told me the scars were moving. She told me the scars were smiling at her.

CHAPTER 11

Breaking the Circle

I'm seven years old and I'm hiding in a cupboard in the kitchen. Dad is out there somewhere, looking for me. I can hear his footsteps.
"Cora!" he shouts.

I don't say a word.

I hear him take something from the worktop. I imagine it's something sharp. He wants to kill me again. The face on Mum's back told him to do it.

I think part of Dad doesn't want to find me when he gets like this. He never checks the cupboards. I decide to believe that this is true and that it's just a game where I hide in a cupboard and Dad pretends he doesn't know I'm in there. It's like our own version of hide and seek except if I lose, he will kill me.

His footsteps pass close by. I hold my breath. There's a sound in the dark. It's not fair if you play too, I think. You can cheat.

"Astaroth," whispers the voice in the dark.

I didn't want to stay in the cupboard with the voice. I didn't want to play at all anymore, but I had to decide.

"Are those scars?" asks Anton, and I remember we're playing a different game now.

He's looking at the raised skin on my back, just beneath the clasp of my bra. I had the tattoos arranged so that they deliberately made the scars difficult to see without actually covering them. It was like an optical illusion on my flesh. You had to be looking for the scars to see them, but once you saw them, you wouldn't be able to see anything else. Jake worked on the tattoo for a year. He didn't understand the other stuff I wanted to add, the symbols and unfamiliar words, but he liked the challenge of hiding the scars without actually hiding them.

The few people who had seen the tattoo had all seen something different. One saw a maze, another a flower, an ex once told me they saw a map.

"It's a face," says Tom, looking away as if he saw the scars immediately, but I know he had been looking for longer than that. I could feel it.

Anton steps closer, bends down to see. I can feel his breath on my back.

Tom moves around in front of me to deliver his diagnosis, "There was something inside your mum and you knew there was because you had it too."

I don't have time to respond to this because Anton shouts, "Fuck!"

He backs away and would have stepped out of the circle, but Tom reaches out and grabs him before he crosses the line.

"What happened?" asks Tom.

"Nothing," says Anton, shaking his head.

"Anton, what did you see?" Tom insists.

Anton continues to shake his head, either because he's declining to answer Tom's question or because he's denying what he saw to himself. I decide to help him out.

"You saw it move."

I pick up my shirt and put it back on because now I know they'll be looking again and I don't like it anymore. I didn't like it to begin with, but it was necessary then. They will believe it's necessary now, but there will be other opportunities.

"Did you?" asks Tom.

Anton thinks for a moment, "I don't think so, it can't have been. A muscle spasm maybe?"

"My dad used to say he saw Mum's scars moving," I say, "He even said they talked to him."

"Coralie, you have to tell me how you got the scars," says Anton, trying to take Tom's place as lead investigator.

"It was after you left," says Tom. "Your mum had them. Your dad, for reasons we don't yet understand, thought they weren't inflicted scars, correct? He thought they were evidence of some kind of demonic possession. You didn't believe him so you left, but then one day you found you had the same scars."

I nod in agreement.

Anton is shaking his head again. "You can't just get scars like that without noticing. They look like knife wounds. No, they're too uneven for that, they're more like scratches. They must have been deep to scar like that."

"When exactly did you notice the scars?" Tom asks.

"It would be about five years ago."

"And you recognised them as the same scars your mum had?"

I nod again.

"So why didn't you come back here?" says Tom and I know where he's going with this because he's always going to stick up for Dad. "Surely the scars were proof that maybe your dad was right. We can dispute his methods and I'm not trying to justify or explain what he did but wasn't there some part of you that wanted to talk to him about? Didn't you consider he may have been able to help you?"

"Help me?" I say, "His idea of helping Mum was to lock her in this room for days at a time. He cut her, he beat her, and he'd started doing the same to me. He knew it was inside me, too. I know that now; I knew it when I discovered the scars, but I couldn't make sense of what he did. You didn't see what he did to us. There are things too awful to talk about; things I've never told anyone."

"Sex magic?" Anton suggests, and the look Tom gives him makes him instantly regret it.

"Don't be ridiculous," he shouts, "No matter what he did this is her father we're talking about."

Standing up for Dad again. I wonder if this is a thing men do, always giving other men the benefit of the doubt while they will condemn a woman in a heartbeat. Of course it is, I don't need to wonder. I suspect it's because Tom sees something of himself in the sketch of my dad he's putting together in his imagination. He's trying to think about what he would do if he had a wife and a daughter and he believed them to be possessed by a demonic entity. How far would he go?

"He's right," I say although it's not strictly true, but Tom's faith in a man he's never met was annoying me. "He had books on sex magic. He'd tried all kinds of things with Mum, even blood rituals. Nothing worked. Her scars were so much worse than mine. The last time I saw her ... I couldn't even tell it was her anymore. The scars took over her whole body, and it was like they'd moved. She had something that looked like a face on her too, but by the end the scars were her face. I don't know how else to explain it."

"I have to be honest," Anton says to Tom, "I've never seen anything like this before. I've seen bruises caused by spirits and I've seen scratches from demonic entities, I've even received scratches myself. I've never seen scars like this."

"Neither have I," says Tom.

"I can't even think of any cases with scars this pronounced," Anton continues.

Tom does this thing with his face where he looks like he's posing for the author photo on a skepticism book.

"So this is the part where you accuse me of making it all up," I say, hoping to beat them to it, "Like the ghost of my dad and the noises and everything else."

"I think we're beyond that now," says Tom, "Although you haven't been entirely honest with us. The tattoos around the scar aren't just to hide it, are they? Those are protective symbols. You've known more about what we do than you've let on."

I nod, but I don't explain. It's obvious, isn't it? Why would they help me otherwise? Anton needed a damsel in distress, Tom needed a willing student. It worked. They're both here.

"You learnt from your dad?" Tom continues.

I nod again. I don't want to go into detail about everything Dad taught me. It makes him seem like he was trying to help me, and that doesn't work with my story. They are also strangely happy memories. We'd sit on the floor of the lounge with his books open, comparing the techniques and symbols of different practitioners. He would show me how to sit when performing a ritual, and he would help me pronounce the words. It was the only real father-daughter time I had with him in those last years before I left and I'm keeping those memories for myself.

"Do they work?" Tom asks.

"If they don't, we're inside a protective circle with a demon," Anton points out, but Tom doesn't acknowledge this.

"Before I had the tattoos, the scars used to hurt sometimes," I admit, "They don't hurt anymore. They stopped growing, too. I haven't lied to you. I just couldn't tell you all of this straight away. There's too much. I was worried you wouldn't believe me and I'm still not sure you do."

"Maybe you haven't lied," Tom agrees, "But you know more about what's happening here than you've told us. I saw some of the same symbols in our circle on your back. You came to us as a naïve innocent with no knowledge of spirits and demons and black magic, and yet the entire time you had evidence to the contrary scratched into your flesh!"

This all seems rather dramatic coming from Tom. He sounds more like his brother at the crescendo of one of the more dramatic episodes of his TV show. Speaking of which, we hadn't heard from the crew for nearly an hour now. Anton's demonologist hadn't arrived. I think about pointing this out but it feels like the wrong time. Anton and Tom are waiting for my big confession. Let's give them what they want.

"I shouldn't have brought you into this," I think is a good place to start, showing a little remorse.

"But you did," says Anton, although they may

as well be speaking as one voice now because their opinions of me have almost completely aligned.

Balance. I wasn't sure it was going to be possible, but here we are, where I need them to be. Once something is balanced, it's much easier to decide which way to tip it over.

"I thought if I could fix this house and expel whatever is in here maybe it would go away forever, but I didn't want to spend my whole life trying to fix it. I wanted one last ritual; one final assault. That's why I needed help."

"Okay, fine," says Anton. "Let's put aside what you did or didn't tell us and what you already know. Let's say this is all true. What is it? What's inside this house? What was it that got inside your mum and then into you?"

I don't know the answer to that, so I wait for Tom to deliver his verdict.

"That's your area of expertise, isn't it?" he says to Anton. "What do you think it is? Pretend the cameras are rolling. What would you say now about what happened in this house?"

"I'm way out of my depth here, Tom."

"I've seen you on TV. There's a new demon every week," says Tom and I half-expect some kind of retort from Anton but he is staring at the floor, "You work with a self-proclaimed demonologist, whatever that is. Didn't you learn anything?"

"I know a few of the names..." Anton replies, but he loses confidence as he says it, probably because he's worried Tom will test him on it.

"You've been scratched by demons," Tom continues. "You were possessed by a demon once. I remember they made such a big deal about that in the promos."

"You were always more into this than I was," Anton admits and it feels like this should be a big moment between them but Tom is still going.

"Paranormal phenomena," he says, "Sounds and movements and visions that are apparently unexplainable until I turn up and explain them. Science. Rational thought. That's what I'm into. You're telling me this is something else. Fine, I'll go along with it, but you need to take the lead. What is it you say in your stage show? There's a war going on out there in the dark."

"Tom, stop—"

"You know the rest. I'm not a ghost hunter, you say. I'm a warrior and I'm bringing the fight to them. So bring it. This woman needs your help. She has a demon, not inside, but apparently it's on the outside and it's looking at you. What are you going to do, Anton? What are you going to do?"

"What do you want me to say?" Anton asks, "That I made some of that stuff up? Yeah, of course I did, but not all of it. Things happened I couldn't explain just like I can't explain what I just saw."

"No," Tom shakes his head. "It was all invented, wasn't it? This is important. If we're going to help Coralie, I need you to tell me that all the demons and the possessions and the scratches were set up. We're dealing with something serious so we need to set a baseline. The cameras are off. We never have to speak of this again, but you need to tell me you never believed in demons to begin with."

"You know I can't do that," Anton says. "I was there, remember? That first time, I was therre."

Tom looks like Anton just punched him on the nose. Nothing he just said had any bearing on today. He simply spotted a weakness in Anton's armour, and he went for it. Tom said all the things he's been wanting to say for years. I can picture him watching Anton on TV, then pacing up and down as he prepares the counter-argument he knows he will never deliver. In the end, he didn't need to argue with anything, he just needed to see that Anton was afraid and that was enough. I suspect Tom thought Anton would break down and confess all his sins, but he hit back.

"We were children," says Tom, with a finality that suggests this is all he wants to say on the matter.

I know what they're talking about. It's the abandoned house story Anton told in his show where he was locked in a room with a demonic entity. If it happened the way Anton described, then their relationship makes sense. Tom would have to be torn apart by his guilt at leaving Anton in that house, and Anton would never have forgiven his brother for doing it. Anton becomes obsessed with what happened to him in that room and pursues an interest in the paranormal in order to uncover the truth. Driven by guilt, Tom takes the opposite path and dedicates his life to debunking ghost stories in order to prove to himself that Anton wasn't in all that much danger after all. It makes sense, but I want to be certain.

"What happened?"

"It was a long time ago," says Anton, looking at Tom hoping he will respond for him.

"Nothing happened," says Tom.

"You can't believe that," Anton argues, stunned.

They never talked about it. This one pivotal event sent them off on different paths and they never thought to discuss how they felt about it. They both thought the other felt the same way. Anton thought Tom was on the same truth-seeking path he was, even if his methods were different. That means Tom must have thought Anton believed nothing had happened either. I want more, but I can see I won't get it from Tom.

"Memories are slippery," Tom explains. "I can't say for certain anything happened to us then and I can't say for certain anything is happening now."

Tom looks at me as he says this and I know he's deliberately changing the subject, so I shout, "You still don't believe me! After all of this. You're the one who ran in here, panicked everyone and drew the circle and now you're saying it's all a lie!"

"It's not that simple," he explains, "Belief isn't black-and-white, it's a spectrum. There are things I still don't understand, but I know the intention of the white hen and the black rooster. A bomb scare has to be taken seriously whether or not it's real," he says, with this smug expression like he's been waiting to use that line since he thought of it.

"I refuse to spend my last night in this house debating what I know to be true," I say with confidence but I'm really just masking the fact that I'm making this up as I go along, "I'll prove it to you."

I take a decisive step towards the edge of the circle. It's time to move things forward. I want to see how strong their beliefs really are.

"Don't!" shouts Anton.

"Why? You don't actually believe anything will happen to me, so where's the danger?"

"I believe you," he says, trying to give me his most sincere expression.

"You didn't want me to talk about seeing my dead dad because you thought I'd seem crazy on camera," I remind him. "I don't need you to believe anything. I need it from him."

I look at Tom. He doesn't say a word. I take another step. My left foot is touching the inner circle now.

"Tell her you believe her," Anton orders Tom.

I move my right foot in line with the left.

"I'm not going to lie," says Tom.

I hesitate, considering for the first time that they will not stop me and that I'm actually going to leave the circle.

"So you'll watch her die instead?"

I can see a shape in the corner of the room. It's Dad. Either he was always there all along or being this close to the edge of the circle means I can see him again.

"Nothing will happen to her," Tom states.

I move to take one more step.

"What then?" Anton demands, "What are we even doing here if you don't believe anything will happen out there? What are we protecting ourselves from? What happened downstairs?"

A thought occurs to Tom, and he blinks, then he turns to me.

"Coralie, wait," he says.

It's too late now. I've stepped out of the circle.

CHAPTER 12

While I Was Downstairs

Tom and Anton stare at me, neither really knowing how to react. Dad is standing next to me, and I'm surprised to find I'm relieved to see him. I decide to pack that feeling away to examine later. Now I need to find out what happened downstairs.

I turn and skip towards the door. I don't know why I skipped; I suppose to emphasise my joy at being free of the circle. Looking back, it was a little childish. I don't go downstairs. I go out onto the landing and walk down a few steps, but then I creep back up. The landing is dark and they can't see me, but I can see them. I expect they'll guess I didn't go all the way downstairs, but I'm not sure they have. We've not heard from anyone downstairs for so long it probably seems like I've stepped into a void. They're both just staring at the doorway. I think I've confused them.

"Coralie!" Anton shouts, eventually.

I don't respond.

"Nothing happened," he says.

"She hasn't come back," Tom points out.

I stifle a giggle. I feel like a child playing hide and seek. Neither of them really knows what to do with themselves now I'm not playing their game anymore.

Anton steps to the edge of the circle and tries to pierce the darkness on the other side of the doorway by simply looking at it.

"Nothing happened to her when she stepped out of the circle," he says, "She didn't die."

"I didn't think she would," says Tom, "But something's happened. She went straight to the door and down the stairs without saying a word and now, nothing. Why?"

"Coralie!" Anton shouts again. "What's happening down there?"

I wait in the dark, and I don't make a sound. I wonder what is happening down there? I really want to see. No, I can't look. I need to monitor them. I need to remember why we're all here.

"I'm going to look," Anton says eventually.

"Go ahead," says Tom, daring him to do it.

Anton turns to look at his brother and protests, "You tried to stop her but not me."

"I know you won't do it," Tom states. "You

believe there's something down there. She didn't. You know for a fact the circle protects us. She didn't."

"How can you say she doesn't believe?" asks Anton, but I don't think he really wants an answer. I think he's stalling, "She called us."

"She wanted us to tell her there really were ghosts here. She wanted us to tell her that her parents weren't insane; that her mum wasn't schizophrenic and her dad hadn't treated it with antiquated, violent, black magic rituals. She wanted us to tell her that everything that happened to her happened for a reason. She wanted us to tell her that this shadow that she's been living under her whole life is more than a delusion."

That hurts, Tom.

"I believed her," says Anton, and if I wasn't hiding, I would gift him a small but knowing smile.

"Her dad gave her the scars on her back," says Tom.

"Tom, I saw them move," Anton almost whispers, like he's afraid to admit it.

"Think about what you're saying. You think the scars on her flesh are somehow alive? There's no precedent for that, it's ridiculous. You didn't see them move, they just looked like they were moving because of where they were and how she moved. Maybe she did that on purpose, I don't know. Maybe she practiced it. I certainly didn't see any evidence that the scars were alive."

Anton considers this, then asks, "So you think

her dad did that to her?"

"It's horrible, but yes, because it explains everything. Her dad was a broken, deranged man who, rather than seeking professional help, acted out his delusions on his family. It must have been a hideous childhood and no matter what she does, she can't get away from it because the evidence is scarred into her flesh. But she can make the scars into something else, hence the tattoos, hence the stories, hence her whole life."

He's very good, isn't he? I'm convinced and I know for a fact he's wrong because I can still see my dead dad and he's looking right at me.

"You go then," dares Anton. "You don't believe in it so step out of the circle."

Tom doesn't move. Nice one, Anton. You're right to call him out. I think he's scared. I think maybe he believes in ghosts after all and this whole rationalisation process he goes through is a cover for his own fears and superstitions. He did see Dad too, after all. He's talked himself out of it but he can't deny what he saw.

"This is ridiculous," says Anton, and he steps towards the edge of the circle again.

"I believe a black magic ritual took place here before we started," says Tom, stopping Anton in his tracks, "Whether it involves Coralie or not I think there may be danger outside the circle. I hope I'm wrong. I'd love to be wrong. I'm not leaving until I know for sure. If you want to leave you go ahead."

"How can you be afraid of something you don't believe in?" Anton asks.

"I'm not afraid, but I don't have all the facts. Here are the facts I do have. Someone sacrificed two birds outside this house. I don't believe the sacrifice itself has power but I believe whoever did that believes it does. Something has happened to your crew. Despite your faith in them, I don't know that they're not faking. I don't know that this whole thing isn't for my benefit, but that's just it. I don't know. What if Coralie isn't working alone? What if there is some kind of cult presence here and that's what we're dealing with? Whether it's paranormal or manmade, there is danger here and I'm not ready to confront that danger until I know what it is."

It's an interesting theory. I like the idea that maybe I'm part of some black magic cult. In some ways I wish it were true. It would have made things easier.

Anton still isn't leaving. He walks around the inner perimeter of the circle, pacing a few steps one way, then turning and pacing a few steps back. Tom moves to the opposite side of the circle, the one nearest the window. He stands on his tiptoes and tries to see down into the garden, but he's too far away from the glass and can't quite get the angle. When he gives up and turns around, he sees Anton unbuttoning his shirt.

"What are you doing?" asks Tom.

"I'm going to shake things up."

"With a striptease? I haven't seen your show for a while, I'll admit, but is that what you have to do for viewing figures these days?"

That's a lie. Not the part about viewing figures, but the part about not watching Anton's show. I think Tom watches it every night. I think he tells himself he's secretly proud of his little brother and that helps him pretend he's not at all wallowing in his own jealousy. I think he watches Anton's show and screams abuse at the TV then goes online to debunk every last detail in the fan forums, but we've established that already, we're on the same page here.

"It riles up the spirits," says Anton as he takes off his shirt and drops it onto the floor. "If there's anything here, we'll know about it soon enough. If not, we can walk out of here."

Anton throws his arms into the air. But the performance is for Tom, so he has his back to me. I see something I'm not going to tell you about yet. I know something you don't know!

"Come on!" Anton shouts to the ceiling, "Show yourselves! Is that all you've got? You think banging on a couple of pipes is enough to scare us? Let's see what you look like! Get the fuck out here now!"

Tom shakes his head in mock disdain. "Has this ever worked?"

"Just wait," says Anton, lowering his arms.

There are a few moments of silence. It's an unusually intimate moment with Anton standing topless in my dad's bedroom and my dad inches away from his chest. The silence feels warm and comforting. I could live in this moment forever.

"There's nothing here," Anton declares.

With that, he picks up his shirt and steps out of the circle. That's when Tom sees it and the look on his face is perfect. If he wasn't scared before, he's certainly scared now.

"Anton!"

Anton, now outside the circle, turns back to face his brother and I have a much better view of his naked back this time. I'll tell you what I saw before and what Tom just saw, although you can probably see it yourself now. There are three deep, red scratches across Anton's back in the shape of a face.

CHAPTER 13

A Ghost Story

"There's something on your back," says Tom and there's forced restraint in his voice like he was trying not to scream.

Anton looks at Tom, appearing concerned for a moment. If the scars are causing him any pain, he doesn't appear to feel it. He shakes his head as if Tom's words are a sticky substance he can shake off.

"Give it up, Tom," he says, "There's nothing here."

Still, Anton remains in the room but outside the circle. He's trying to convince himself as much as he's trying to convince Tom. He shuffles closer towards the door as a show of intent.

"It's not in the room," argues Tom, "It's in you."

Again Anton stops to consider this. His right hand moves to his back as if to check for scars, but he hesitates. I wonder if he can feel the scars after all? I wonder if he just doesn't want to admit that he can feel them? If he can feel something on his back, then he knows what that means. I think he's afraid to confront the truth of the situation; I think he's afraid to believe. This surprises me. I'm thinking I had Tom and Anton mixed up. Perhaps Tom is the believer and Anton is the cynic after all.

"You need to leave this room," says Anton, and it's more like a command than a suggestion.

"No," says Tom, folding his arms across his chest like an obstinate child.

"You can't stay here forever. Come on, let's go downstairs."

Anton takes a step away from the door and back towards his brother. Tom reacts like he's taken a slap in the face, dropping to his knees and scrambling for his rucksack. He takes the hammer he used earlier from the bag.

"What do you need that for?" asks Anton, his tone light, but he has stopped in his tracks.

Tom doesn't respond. He's looking for something else in the bag. He takes out a cheap, plastic flask with what looks like water inside.

"Tom?"

Anton takes another step towards his brother but stops at the outer edge of the circle. I wonder if he can cross back into the circle now. I'd like to see him try. I had no trouble crossing the chalk perimeter, but I have protection. I want to know if the magic works. What will crossing the circle do to Anton and the thing inside him? What will Anton do to Tom when nothing happens? What will Tom do to Anton when he's inside the circle?

Tom is on his feet again and brandishing the hammer he shouts, "Stay away from me!"

"Calm it down," says Anton. "Let's go downstairs, find the others and talk this through."

"I know it's not you," says Tom. "Anton would've been out the door by now."

Tom is further ahead in his thinking than I gave him credit. He saw the scars and took that to mean Anton has the same demon inside him that is inside me, which makes sense because the configuration of the scars is similar. As Tom seems to have forsaken his role of professional skeptic for now, I consider the possibility that Anton caused the scars to appear, like when professional wrestlers secretly cut themselves during a match to make it look like their opponent has drawn blood. It's possible he could have scratched himself when Tom wasn't looking but if the wounds are self inflicted, it's very impressive. There wasn't much time for him to do it after seeing my scars, but if he fakes the paranormal activity on his TV show, then I suppose he must have a talent for spotting such opportunities and acting on them quickly. I'm surprised Tom hasn't at least voiced this opinion as a possibility.

Then again, the cameras are no longer recording so who is this performance for? Surely Anton wouldn't waste a moment as big as this on his brother? Perhaps the cameras are recording. Beth left the room with the primary camera, but they put up smaller cameras to monitor to the room. I hadn't considered this before, but it's perfectly plausible that we're all still a part of Anton's show. That's a nice thought, to be honest. I indulge it for a moment.

I walk downstairs. Chloe, Beth, Lee and Steve are huddled round the monitors in the nerve centre. Chloe scowls at me, but Steve gives me a conspiratorial look and places a finger to his lips to indicate I should keep their secret. I join them at the monitor, stifling the giggles caused simply by the act of doing something I know I shouldn't be doing. There's a sense that we're building up to a finale. I imagine Beth has a series of switches in front of her that were responsible for all the noises in the room. There's a big red button, and she's about to press it. She invites me to push it for them, given that it's my house. My finger hovers over the button...

"I don't know what you're talking about," Anton protests. "Just come with me. We don't have to stay in the house; we can go get a pint somewhere. You need a break. We all do."

"You know I can't do that."

"Nothing will happen," Anton continues. "There's nothing in this house. I knew there wasn't from the moment I walked in. The house is empty.

I didn't want it to be true, so I played along. We used to do that anyway, even back when the show was number one."

"Are you admitting you're a fake?" Tom asks, lowering the hammer. Which makes me wonder if this truth bomb is a tactic from Anton.

I'm convinced now that Anton faked the scars, but he's backtracking. He can see he's gone too far. I imagine looking across at Steve with concern. He feels it too, but my finger is still ready to press the big red button.

"Not all the time," Anton admits, "The thing is the show was expensive back then. Even the basics, travelling across the country with a crew and putting them up in a hotel for a couple of nights and feeding them - it all adds up. You add salaries on top of that and costs spiral. We were independently financed, so we had investors. Those investors wanted evidence of paranormal activity, just like the audience did, but the difference was they were paying for it. So, if they've paid for an investigation and we get there and nothing happens I had to give them something."

Tom shakes his head, "Just go."

"I know what you think of me, but don't pretend this is a new, shocking revelation for you," Anton continues, "And don't pretend you wouldn't have done exactly the same thing. It's easy to watch something on TV and critique it and say what you would have done differently. You don't know how much pressure I was under and how quickly I had to make some of those decisions. It wasn't all fake. We captured some genuinely compelling evidence. The problem was once we'd started faking bits and pieces it all becomes part of the same thing. Once I'd learned to react a certain way, it was hard not to apply the same reaction to anything and everything that happened. We lost perspective. Nothing's changed. I still have investors. Not as many as before, but I have people to please and they'll want to see something. I thought you really had something with the circle, but it's gone on for too long now. We need to take a break and think up something else."

Tom raises the hammer again, no longer scared of Anton but disgusted at his suggestion.

"Get out!" Tom shouts.

I press the big red button and watch for the fireworks.

"I'm not leaving you here," says Anton. "I won't do that to you again."

Again. There's a story here. Would you like to hear it? I forgot, you've already heard it. You heard Anton's version though. I forgot to mention that Tom wrote about it too, in the book he self-published to rival Anton's autobiography. Anton's book briefly topped the bestseller lists. Tom's book sold a mere three copies, but one of those was to me. This is how Tom tells the story in his book.

Tom is ten years old. Anton is eight. There's a house not far from their home. It's an old house, and it looks creepy. One day Anton begs Tom to go exploring in the old house. They often go exploring in the neighbourhood together. It was a different time, and things were safer then. Tom eventually agrees and the two of them go to the house.

The house is falling apart. The garden is overgrown. No one has lived there for decades. Squatters have taken residence on and off over the years but they never stay for long. It's not a friendly house. Tom writes that just by looking at the house you could tell bad things happened there once. He says he was the first to go inside, but he admits he felt an intense fear as he approached the building.

They break in through the back door where the wooden frame is loose and splintered and offers no resistance. Inside, the house smells of excrement and rotten timber. The windows have been boarded up, so it's dark. They can't see what they're stepping on. Tom writes about his concern that the house was in fact teeming with life and that he could hear rats in the walls and feel cobwebs brush across his face.

They venture upstairs. The window up there hasn't been boarded, so there's light coming through onto the landing. The stairs creak. Tom describes the creaking as old wood at breaking point.

At the top of the stairs, they find a closed door. After a cursory exploration of the other rooms reveals nothing, they come back to this door. They try to force it open and after some considerable effort it moves. The room beyond is black.

Tom steps into the room and he knows instantly there is someone or something else in there with him. Then Anton shuts the door. He hears his brother run downstairs, laughing. Tom isn't laughing. Tom tries the door, but it's stuck again. He can't move it on his own. He hears something move in the room. He can smell it now. He can feel its hot breath on the back of his neck. Something sharp touches the skin on his arm, followed by more sharp somethings. He screams.

Tom doesn't really remember what happened after that. Anton came back when he heard Tom screaming. He could tell from the sound that Tom was in genuine distress. He says he saw nothing in the room when he opened the door, just Tom on the floor by the door. Tom's fingers were bleeding from scratching at the door to open it from the inside. Tom remembers nothing between the thing touching him and Anton dragging him out of the house into the daylight. He remembers the pain in his arm. He remembers the scratches.

At night he remembers more. He wakes Anton in the next room and he tells his brother what he saw in the dark. A monster. A demon. A name branded on his soul. Astaroth.

CHAPTER 14

Truth Bleeds

"I've read your book," says Tom and though he doesn't need to say he it he continues, "You took my story."

"I know," Anton admits easily, "I'm sorry."

"Are you?"

Anton opens his mouth, presumably to lie, then he closes it again, thinks for a moment and says, "No, I'm not."

Tom throws his arms up in the air in mock defeat. He has to make a show of how much he expected that answer that to cover how hurt he is.

"I was there," Anton continues. "It was my story, too. I changed some details but then, so did you."

"I changed nothing!" Tom screams back. "I've

always told the truth about what happened in that house. It's my story. That story made me who I am. It set the course for the rest of my life and you took it."

"I am sorry for what I did to you," Anton admits. "I should never have left. I think about that moment all the time. When I can't sleep at night, it's not ghosts or demons keeping me awake, it's the memory of your cries for help as I ran down the stairs laughing. I can still see the expression on your face when Dad opened the door. I should never have left you and I regret that moment every day of my life because it changed you and it changed us. Our childhood ended that day."

"You're jealous. You wish what happened to me in there had happened to you, not that it matters. You took the story anyway."

"I'm telling you, I wouldn't wish that on anyone," says Anton, again avoiding Tom's accusation that he stole his experience.

"We both know that's a lie," Tom continues, "Your whole constructed narrative revolves around this thing that didn't even happen to you. I've heard you talk about it in interviews, on stage, on TV... It's all part of the narrative that makes up Anton de Vane, world's greatest paranormal investigator. Where did you get that stupid fucking name, anyway? I get it, Anthony Burgess isn't the most mystical name in the world but at least it's the truth. Everything about you is a lie."

Anton, we're going to keep calling him Anton

because I can't imagine him as Anthony now, nods in agreement and confesses, "In the first draft of my book I wrote the story exactly as it happened. I told myself your experiences were enough of a catalyst for the narrative I was constructing for Anton de Vane. It was my editor who questioned it first. She said the story was too awful and that it made me look bad. She suggested either I cut it down or I cut it out of the book entirely. I stalled on finishing the book for a month, not sure how to move past that one note from my editor. Then, one day, I decided just to try something. Technology makes these things so easy now. I used the 'find and replace' function and with a couple of key-strokes it was done. The story happened to me and not to you."

Tom nods along, but he's not finished. "The worst part is you make it out to be this tran-scendent moment; a spiritual epiphany. It wasn't anything like that. It was worse than anything you could imagine. I've never really been able to de-scribe how terrifying what happened to me was. There was something in that room with me."

"I know," Anton nods, suddenly calm.

"No, you don't. You have no idea. It wasn't a 'presence'. It wasn't a theoretical demon, it was an actual creature. I can still remember the stink of its breath, the feel of its claws as it touched me. It was like an animal, but it spoke. It walked on two legs. I couldn't see much in the dark, but I saw its face... I see that face every time I close my eyes at night.

That's why I'm a skeptic, Anton. That's why I don't believe in ghosts and poltergeists and all that other horror film rubbish. I encountered something real in that room. I saw evil and evil saw me. I'd know it if I saw it again but I haven't. Not once. I don't believe in your polite ghosts and your TV demons because I've seen something real and something so much worse."

Anton waits for a moment, allowing Tom a minute to catch his breath.

"You don't know what really happened in that house," he says eventually.

"What do you mean?"

"I thought someone would've told you, but I suppose we never spoke about it again. None of us did."

"Told me what?"

Anton hesitates, weighing his words.

"When you didn't come home," he begins, "Mum made me tell her what I'd done."

"Didn't come home?" asks Tom. "You came back and got me."

Anton shakes his head, "You were in that house for two days."

"No, that's not possible."

"At first when you didn't come home I was so scared I'd be in trouble I didn't tell anyone. I said you'd gone out on your own. This is the part I can never forgive myself for, that knowing my brother was in trouble but that there would be consequences for me if anyone found out I chose not to tell anyone. It was like when you break a vase or something and you pick up all the pieces and throw them away and hope no one notices the absence of the vase. I was hoping no one would notice the absence of you. When the guilt made that approach unbearable, I told myself it was a prank. I thought there was no way you would actually stay in that room for an entire day. I told myself the door wasn't that difficult to open and you would've been able to escape eventually, but now you were trying to get me back by making me think you were still in there. When I spoke to Mum, it had been two days. In my book I said it was only one day, not two. I even put in a fight between Mum and Dad to make it look like they were too preoccupied with their own problems to care about you. I made it look like it was their fault and not mine. I feel bad about that too but they were both gone by the time I wrote the book and the dead don't care."

That last part feels like a final twist of the knife in his brother's back. The dead don't care. He doesn't believe. He never believed.

"The truth is," he continues, "Mum and Dad were frantic. They'd called all your school friends, knocked on the door of every house in the street, but no one had seen you. They called the police. The more things escalated, the more I doubled down on my assertion that I didn't know where you were. I'd lied so many times I'd even convinced myself. It was the policewoman who pried the truth out of me in the end. I suppose she'd seen similar things happen. She didn't treat me like a scared, grieving brother; she talking to me like I was a liar, because she knew. So, two days after I'd locked you in that room I told her and everyone else what had happened."

"It can't have been that long," says Tom, whispering now, "I would have remembered."

"You didn't remember back then. You wouldn't speak for a long time and when you did, it was like it had never happened. So we went along with it. We all pretended it had never happened, which was better for everyone. Better to think that everyone is fine and that one son isn't a lying psychopath and the other isn't broken by trauma. I hadn't even realised you had a version of the story until Blackpool."

I realise now I should have recognised Tom, or at least his voice. The Blackpool video is all over the internet. It comes up on those lists sometimes, like "Worst Heckler Ever" or something. It's a video from one of Anton's early live shows. It was when his TV show was at peak popularity so there's a vast audience in this grand concert hall. Anton is telling the story about the house. A man stands up in the audience and accuses him of stealing the story. The man seems drunk and mostly incoherent. Ushers drag him out as he screams, "Liar!" at the top of his voice. I realise now that man was Tom.

"Two days?" Tom asks, but he already knows the answer.

Anton nods once for yes.

"Were you there? When they opened the door, were you there, Anton?"

"We don't have to do this here. It's been a long day. Let's grab a beer and I'll go over the whole thing."

"What did you see?" Tom demands.

"Tom, please—"

"You said I was wrong about what I saw in that room. What did you see!"

"I didn't want to tell you like this. We should get out of here."

"I'm not leaving this circle until you tell me what you saw when you opened the door of that room."

Anton looks at Tom and struggles to decide. I suspect he's weighing up how truly broken his relationship with his brother really is against how he thought this conversation would pan out. I'm sure he always intended to tell Tom the truth one day, but he never imagined it would be in a stranger's house that his brother is afraid to leave. He wipes away a tear. Not now, he must be thinking. There will be time for tears later.

"There was a man in the room with you," Anton says eventually, "He must have been in there when I locked the door."

"It wasn't a man," says Tom, so sure of his memories despite how many of them Anton has already unraveled.

"I think he was homeless. He must have been

using the house for shelter. He was dead by the time we found him."

"There was no one else in that room," Tom insists.

"Mum spoke to the police afterwards. She wanted me to know what had happened. I was eight years old, but she wanted me to know what I'd done to you. I think she thought the guilt would set me straight. In a roundabout way, it did. The man had been alive, maybe twenty-four hours earlier. He'd died of starvation. He didn't look like a human being anymore, just this hairy, skinny creature. I can understand that if you were in the dark and this bony, deranged person was in there with you, there is no way you wouldn't think it was some kind of animal. But he was a man. That's what was in that room with you, Tom. Not a demon, not a monster. A dying man begging for help from a terrified child."

"It's not true," says Tom although he's trying to convince himself now.

"It's true," Anton confirms. "I've known it since that day at the house and I've spent my life in denial because the truth is worse. I don't believe in any of this shit, Tom. Ghosts and demons and magic circles and tapping on the pipes, it's all bullshit. It's stuff we make up because it makes the world seem interesting and helps us ignore the truth. The truth is, we're all just animals scrabbling around for food in the dark. That's all there is. Animals in the dark. It's boring, and it's banal, and it's fucking disgusting sometimes, but it's what we are. When we die, there's nothing. We don't come back. There are no demons, it's just us and our own fucking lies and mistakes. Belief is a choice, the same as lying."

Tom tries one last thing. "What about the screams from downstairs? The sounds?"

"I've worked with this crew for a long time," Anton explains as he points to a camera nestled in the corner of the room. "They would know not to interrupt something like this. I've sacked people for the smallest interruption. They wouldn't risk that. I don't know about the sounds but you know as well as I do that all unusual sounds have a rational explanation. We can review the footage if you like. Maybe you can tell me what happened."

Tom shakes his head. He looks broken. I feel bad for him. Then he looks up at Anton with intent in his eyes.

"This is the demon talking," he says.

"Listen to me," Anton begs. "There are no demons, Tom. There are just people. I know this is hard. I should've told you sooner. Your whole skeptic act was so convincing I thought you knew. I thought you'd figured it out. I didn't know you were acting too."

"I know what you're trying to do here," says Tom, backing away from his brother.

Anton steps forward, crossing the circle again, stepping inside the chalk circumference.

"Tom, please just come with me."

"Get away from me!" Tom shouts.

"I'll drag you out of that circle if it will make you understand."

"I said stay back!"

Tom flips open the cap on the flask he was holding and splashes water on Anton as he steps closer.

"Get out of my brother!" he shouts, as he splashes more water.

Anton knocks the flask out of Tom's hand and then reaches to grab him. He doesn't see Tom swinging his other arm.

There is a wet thud as the hammer impacts the side of Anton's head.

Anton reels from the blow, then staggers back a couple of steps. He lifts a hand to touch the place where Tom hit him, but his probing fingers never reach their destination. Anton drops to the floor.

Tom looks down at his brother and watches as a halo of blood encircles Anton's head then spreads from the centre of the circle outwards. Anton is dead.

CHAPTER 15

Astaroth

Tom is on his knees now, shaking Anton's body. Tears run down his cheeks and the odd drop splashes into the pool of red on the floor.

"Anton, get up!" Tom shouts, desperate. "It's over. I saved you. We can leave!"

Tom shakes Anton a few more times. Anton's body is limp and unresponsive. I've never really seen a body so soon after death. I didn't realise how obvious it would be that they are dead. You can tell by the way Anton's body responds to Tom's attempts at revival. It's hard to put my finger on exactly what gives it away, but it just seems so clear that there is no life in that body anymore.

Tom shakes Anton for a little while longer and

then he realises what has happened and what he has done. He sits back and shuffles to the perimeter of the circle again, his eyes never leaving his dead brother's body. As he moves away, he realises he's still holding the hammer. He throws it across the room as if it's going to explode in his hands.

There is a sound from above. It starts as a few taps like before, but then it becomes something else. It sounds like a low growl.

Tom looks up at the ceiling for a moment and then back down at Anton's body. He's seen something. He crawls over to inspect the widening pool of blood and notices a line where it has seeped through a join in the laminate flooring. I don't know what makes him do it, maybe it's something from his insurance inspection training or maybe he just wants to break something but he pushes his fingers under the edge of the laminate and lifts it up. He looks underneath and I can tell from the way his expression changes that whatever his suspicions were, they have been confirmed.

Tom gets to work on the floor. He has a job now, and the renewed sense of purpose must have pushed the horror of what he did to the back of his mind. He grabs Anton by the ankles and drags his lifeless body to the corner of the room as if he were a piece of furniture. With the largest obstacle removed, Tom sets about packing away his equipment. He moves over to the window and somehow lifts the rusted latch and pushes the window open. Sounds of birdsong and traffic invade the silent room. Tom collects the silver cups of water one at a time and empties their contents out of the window before packing them away in his bag. He blows out the candles and packs them away too, along with any other bits and pieces that ended up on the floor after his hurried preparation of the circle. With everything packed away and his dead brother out of sight, Tom takes up the floor.

As he works, I look up at the camera Anton pointed out earlier. There have been no sounds from downstairs, which debunks Anton's theory that the crew are simply staying out of his way for fear of reprisal should they interrupt a paranormal event in progress. Surely they wouldn't refrain from interrupting now? Perhaps they wouldn't come upstairs to confront the man who has murdered their employer but it would be reasonable to expect some activity. I know why there's no reaction from them, obviously, but I'm surprised Tom hasn't considered it. Then again, I suppose to him it's further evidence that he was right all along.

The laminate hasn't been stuck down and comes away easily. Having pulled up a large section of the floor covering, Tom looks down at the wooden boards beneath and sees what he expected to see. He continues to work, rolling up each section of laminate in his hands and then piling them on top of Anton's body. He is calm and methodical and in his element. Finally, when most of the floor covering has been pulled up and the floorboards beneath are fully exposed, Tom steps back and surveys what he has revealed.

Drawn in white paint on the floorboards is another circle with a pentagram inside, although the markings and words in the outer circle are different. This second circle is the same size and sits in almost exactly the same position as the circle Tom drew on top of it.

The low growl from above is louder now, the tapping becomes a more insistent sound of knuckles knocking on wood. Tom doesn't notice. He's staring at the circle and trying to decipher the inscriptions. He reaches into his bag searching for something, then takes out a book. Flipping through the pages, he decides it's the wrong book, packs it away and takes out another. This one provides the answers he's looking for. He matches the inscriptions in the circle on the floorboards to the diagram in the pages of his book.

"It's a binding circle," he says to no one in particular.

I decide he may as well be saying it to me, and so I step back into the room.

Tom looks up as I enter, and the professionalism disappears. I had allowed him to take back a small amount of control, but now I'm taking it away again. There's a hopelessness in his expression, but it is without guilt for the moment. I wonder if I should have given him more time to take in what he's done, but I wouldn't be able to wait much longer, anyway. I'm too excited about what is about to happen.

"There was something inside him," says Tom.

"There was something inside my mum too," I begin. "A demon, I suppose you'd call it. I'm not sure that word really explains anything, but it will do for now. Dad spent most of his life trying to get it out of her. In the end he gave up."

Tom is looking over his shoulder at Anton now, and I can see he is beginning to understand. I don't think he's even listening to me.

"I killed him," he says.

"You did," I agree, "You killed him the moment you stepped into this room."

He looks at me again now and asks, "What do you mean?"

"Dad decided the only way to stop the demon was to kill Mum. The demon wouldn't let him. It was too powerful for that. So, he locked mum in the loft and drew this circle to keep her there."

I point to the newly revealed circle on the floor that Tom had correctly identified as a binding circle.

"She wasn't able to leave," I continue, "He thought eventually she would die from starvation or dehydration but she didn't. The problem with the circle was that it prevented the demon from leaving too, and it wouldn't let her die. I don't know if there's anything left of Mum anymore, to be honest. I suspect she's just a corpse with a monster inside it, puppeteering the limbs to bang on the floor."

A couple of bangs from above would be great right now, but there's only silence. Thanks for nothing.

Tom's eyes follow the line of the circle. He notices the pool of Anton's blood in the dead centre. He reads some of the inscriptions again and consults his book. Finally, he understands.

"You wanted this to happen."

"The thing inside my mum could get into other people too, as long as they were inside the circle. But it's not how you think; they don't jump from body to body like fleas. They split and multiply, like a virus."

"My name is Legion," Tom recites, "for we are many."

I allow him his little movie trailer moment before I continue. "Dad made such a big deal about me never setting foot inside this room. Obviously, I had to find a way in. I wanted to see mum. She used to call to me in the night. So one day I stole Dad's key, and I came in here. That was the day the thing inside Mum found its way inside me."

I don't intend to look at Dad, but I sense a movement so I turn and I see him sobbing. There is no sound and no tears, but he has his face in his hands and his shoulders are jolting up and down as he cries. For the first time, I consider the possibility that this projection of my dad is actually part of my dad. It's too late, though. I need to finish the story.

"Dad did everything he could to get it out, that

part was true, although he couldn't bring himself to hurt me the way he'd hurt Mum."

"Didn't he go to anyone for help?" Tom asks because I've obviously not made it clear enough that this is a time for listening.

"Once it was inside me I became bound by the circle too," I explain. "That's what Dad said. I suppose I never tested it. I just knew I couldn't leave. Dad convinced a couple of people to come here to look, but they were like you two. People just want stories for their books or their YouTube channel; no one really wants to help."

I expect Tom to protest against me lumping him in with his brother and had it been the other way around, I'm sure Anton would have had something to say about it. Tom doesn't flinch. He knows why he came here.

Tap-tap-tap. There you are. About time.

"Then Dad had the bright idea of binding the demon to my flesh," I continue. "He saw the face in the scars and he thought maybe he could limit its power over me. It was tough to find someone who would do it. I heard him on the phone trying to convince these seaside tattoo artists to come over and ink his teenage daughter. He would have to go into the whole thing about how I was trapped in his bedroom and how I probably wouldn't want the tattoo, but how it was a matter of life or death. You can imagine how that would sound. Then he found Jake, the only tattoo artist on the South Coast without a conscience."

"What did it feel like?" Tom asks.

"It fucking hurt!"

"Not the tattoo. The demon. What did it feel like to have something like that inside you?"

"Don't you know?"

Tom looks down at his gut, which strikes me as weird, but I suppose if you think something bad is inside you, then that's the first place you think of. He looks up at me again with concern.

"My name is Legion," I say, "for we are many."

He knows.

"What does it want?" he asks.

"I don't know what it wants now," I admit, "Before, it wanted Dad to kill me. It would make me provoke him. I said all kinds of awful things."

I can't look at Dad anymore. I remember some of the things I said and despite where we are now and what's about to happen, I can't help feeling more than a little ashamed.

Tom is looking at the circle again.

"Blood magic," he says.

I nod and finish his thought for him. "The blood of someone killed by family. Blood spilled by blood. That was what would unlock the circle."

The tapping is now a loud knocking. It's okay. We're nearly done.

"He sent you away, didn't he," says Tom as he puts the last of the pieces together.

"Either the tattoos did their job or the tattooing my dad commissioned counted as enough spilt blood to break the circle. That's what he told me, and once I was out, I was out. He sent me away."

"Was it the demon inside you that brought you back here, or did you decide that on your own?"

The knocking is now a banging. It's too much. We haven't finished talking.

"I didn't think you believed in demons, Tom," I say. "There's nothing that happened here today that couldn't have been set up or couldn't be explained. I could've planted the dead birds. Making sure you found them wouldn't have been difficult, not if I had help. The crew could have been in on it. Poor Anton could have been in on it too, although I don't think he's going to leap to his feet and yell 'surprise'. I think we're past that point now."

The banging is at the door to the loft now. The circle has indeed been broken. Tom is looking at the door.

"What's behind the door?"

The banging is so loud and violent now it sounds like the door will be forced open.

Okay, I've done my part. It's your turn now, Mum.

"What's behind the door?!"

You wrest the door from its hinges and send it flying across the room. He looks at you, scared but also understanding that you've been up there the whole time and now he's broken the circle you're free. I watch as you lumber across the floor, your body broken, your flesh rotten, but the thing inside you is alive and it moves.

Tom screams as you descend on him. Your face

is death and though he tries to look away, he's already seen too much. You devour him. I leave you to it.

Downstairs I find Jake in the kitchen, still holding the bloodstained knife he used to silence the crew. He looks at me to ask if we're done, but doesn't say the words. He doesn't need to. The thing inside me hears the thing I put inside him.

"We're done," I say.

I open the door and I leave my house again. As I walk along the street, I turn for one last look. Dad is standing outside, but he's not following. He'll never follow me again.

EPILOGUE

I finish making Anton look pretty. His eyes have begun to dehydrate in their sockets, so I place the eye caps under the shriveling lids to keep them closed. Most mortuary assistants like to do the eye caps first so they don't have to look into the eyes of their subject while they work. I always leave the eyes until last. That's how I hear their stories.

I never think about whether the stories are true. Maybe the dead lie as much as the living do. It's not for me to decide. I have wondered about my part in the stories and how much of the story comes from me. Does it matter? What matters is there was something inside this body that didn't belong. It's not part of the job description but would I really be doing my job if I didn't take the proper precautions? We don't fully seal caskets because the decomposition process can cause them to explode. I feel it is only right to approach a body that has been host to a parasite with the same level of caution. However, if anyone found out about me doing this, I would probably lose my job. This is why I work alone.

Carefully, I unbutton Anton's shirt and expose his chest. I use a scalpel to cut a circle into the flesh and then I add my own words into the outer circle. I include Astaroth, because naming is important but otherwise my circle is based on an older and more powerful design than the one employed by poor Tom Burgess.

I button up the shirt so no one will know and I step back and survey Anton lying there in his suit with his face plastered with make-up and his hair styled in the way he used to have it on TV. He looks like he's part of a show now, only this time he's the volunteer and I'm the magician. Tomorrow there will be an audience and we'll make him disappear. Unfortunately, I can't bring him back. That really would be a magic trick worth seeing.

I go to the funeral. People don't always want me there. No one wants to think about what I do to the bodies; they want to believe the person fell down dead looking like they did when they last saw them and that's how they will always appear, preserved for all time. As long as I keep to myself and don't talk to the mourners, they assume I'm an old friend or distant relative. I wear large sunglasses so no one can see I'm not crying. Once, an upset and rather drunk mourner demanded to know who I was, and I just did my best theatrical sob and walked away. There were no follow-up complaints.

There aren't many at Anton's funeral. His parents are no longer around or unable to travel and he doesn't appear to have had many friends. He was the kind of celebrity you forget about the moment they're off the TV for more than a week. I wondered if the manner of his death might bring him some post-humus attention, but no one seems to care. We are also a long way from where Anton lived and died, but mine always are. I don't know why.

On the way home, I see a man watching the funeral from afar. I don't know who he is and Anton is in the ground now so he can't tell me but I decide the man is Tom. I decide Tom escaped the clutches of whatever was in the loft and though part of it is inside him now, perhaps he has made peace with that. Maybe this is how the ghost-hunting brothers save the world from evil in the end. They keep their demons to themselves.

At home I sit in the dark, and I write up my story. I worry I'm not supposed to do this. The stories are a gift, so you could say they belong to me, but are they truly mine to share? I tell myself I have to get them out otherwise they will consume me.

I post the story on my blog, and I read a little before going to bed. As I'm about to switch off my laptop, I notice an email informing me of a new comment. I usually close the blog to comments but I must have forgotten to tick the box.

"You did well today," the comment reads, "We

look forward to seeing you again soon."

Trolls, I think. Spam bots. Ignore, delete, move on.

As I close my eyes I can't help thinking, maybe it wasn't Tom at the funeral. Maybe it was someone else. I look at the email again, wondering if the commenter left a name. They did.

Asmodeus.

IF YOU ENJOYED
THIS BOOK...

If I can convince Coralie the books are successful then she will hopefully give me more stories. To this end, please consider leaving a review on Amazon or Goodreads or even talking about the book on social media.

To hear about future releases (and to receive a free copy of the first book in the Jenny Ringo series) sign up to the mailing list at:

www.peopleinthedark.com

ABOUT THE AUTHOR

Chris Regan

Chris Regan was born and raised in Stoke-on-Trent. He graduated with a Masters degree in Creative Writing from the University of East Anglia. Chris has written scripts for four feature films that  have been released internationally. His credits include: Ten Dead Men, London Heist and most recently Paintball Massacre. His movies have been seen on Netflix, Sky Cinema and UK TV, where they continue to gain a following and appreciation.

Additionally, Chris has made several short films as well as the acclaimed and controversial web series Paz vs Stuff.

Chris lives in Worthing.

BOOKS BY THIS AUTHOR

The Library Of Lost Souls

Slacking university student Gavin wants nothing more than to spend his days reading anything other than his course materials and getting out of having to study – and for him, hiding out in the dusty halls of the library is the perfect place to do it.

But when he notices his fellow students are all missing a pretty important feature, Gavin soon realizes that something has gone seriously wrong. After a hectic escape causes him to stumble into amateur witch Jenny Ringo, Gavin finds himself falling headlong into a world of chaotic spells, horrific hexes, and Jenny's half-baked attempts to set things right.

But undoing such serious magic is no easy feat. Short of selling her soul to demons, Jenny and Gavin will need to work together and use all their wits if they want to fix their fellow students before anyone else finds out...

The House Party From Hell

After the last time she tried and failed to use her magic, amateur witch Jenny Ringo has quit magic altogether for a simpler life with a nine to five job. Unfortunately, she and her flatmate and friend, Gavin have discovered there's something strange going on in their building.

Having no ability to conjure spells himself, Gavin is convinced it's time for Jenny to use her powers to help them, even though Jenny is trying to live her life enchantment free. Unable to get out of the building, tensions between the friends run high, so they accept an invite to a party happening at another resident's flat.

Once they begin meeting the neighbors, they realize there's more to the people next door than they thought. As they plunge deeper into a dangerous world of vampires, werewolves, and magic they don't understand, Gavin has to convince Jenny her spells are the key to their salvation.

Christmas Chopping

Christmas is in the air, but for amateur witch Jenny Ringo and her best friend Gavin, the scares are only just getting started. It turns out that the festive season is the perfect time for all the monsters, ghosts and ghouls to leave their lairs and roam the now-empty streets.

Eager to meet their less-then-human neighbours, the pair take to their home city of Brighton to soak in the spooky atmosphere. There's only one problem – they're warned to go home before it gets dark, otherwise the infamous Spider Claws will find them.

You see, monsters and ghosts have a very interesting version of Santa Claus. One who likes to hide in the dark and ensnare unsuspecting shoppers with his silky webs – and when Jenny and Gavin's friend Casper falls into the lair of this alarming arachnid, they'll need to act fast if they want to save him before he ends up facing a very ghastly fate indeed...

CORALIE WESTERLY
WILL RETURN IN....

ASMODEUS

Printed in Great Britain
by Amazon

67063138R00127